BACKLIGHT

BACKLIGHT

PIRKKO SAISIO

TRANSLATED FROM FINNISH BY MIA SPANGENBERG

TWO LINES
PRESS

Originally published as *Vastavalo*
Copyright © 2000 by Pirkko Saisio
Published originally in Finnish by WSOY
Published in agreement with Helsinki Literary Agency and Regal Hoffmann and Associates
Translation copyright © 2025 by Mia Spangenberg

Two Lines Press
582 Market Street, Suite 700, San Francisco, CA 94104
www.twolinespress.com

ISBN: 978-1-949641-80-6
Ebook ISBN: 978-1-949641-81-3

Cover Design by Rafael Nobre
Typeset by schubet

The line "the stones are shifting in the Moldau, and three Kaisers are dead and buried in Prague" on pages 1 and 2 is from "Das Lied von der Maldau" by Bertolt Brecht.

Library of Congress Cataloging-in-Publication Data
Names: Saisio, Pirkko, 1949- author. | Spangenberg, Mia M., translator.
Title: Backlight / Pirkko Saisio ; translated from Finnish by Mia Spangenberg.
Other titles: Vastavalo. English
Description: San Francisco, CA : Two Lines Press, 2025.
Identifiers: LCCN 2024054721 (print) | LCCN 2024054722 (ebook) | ISBN 9781949641806 (hardback) | ISBN 9781949641813 (ebook)
Subjects: LCSH: Saisio, Pirkko, 1949---Fiction. | LCGFT: Autobiographical fiction. | Bildungsromans. | Queer fiction. | Novels.
Classification: LCC PH355.S2146 V3713 2025 (print) | LCC PH355.S2146 (ebook) | DDC 894/.54133--dc23/eng/20241120
LC record available at https://lccn.loc.gov/2024054721
LC ebook record available at https://lccn.loc.gov/2024054722

1 3 5 7 9 10 8 6 4 2

This work has been published with the financial support of FILI - Finnish Literature Exchange and is supported in part by an award from the National Endowment for the Arts.

It's 5 a.m. and the world is cast in gold.

Shimmering fog lies tangled in the willows an excavator will lift from the earth years later. Water beads on the untroubled grass, wild just moments ago.

She's backlit by the sun.
She's crossing the meadow toward me.

In a few years a Citymarket will be built here, and the meadow will be paved so families will have a place to park their Toyotas, Datsuns, and Labrador retrievers on Saturdays.

But there's still time until then, a little.

Now it's 1968, Europe's crazy year, and that crazy summer is about to begin.
Vanha, the Old Student House, won't be occupied until autumn, but there will be riots in Paris over the summer. Tanks are lining up in Moscow, the stones are

shifting in the Moldau, and three Kaisers are dead and buried in Prague.
There are three bullets lying in wait in Josef Bachmann's gun, Rudi Dutschke is laid out in his bed, and a cow lies in the meadow she's crossing toward me.

It's 5 a.m. on the first day of June and the world is cast in gold.
She's also dressed in gold, in an ethereal cloak of mist, and I can't see her face.
I recognize her by her hesitant footsteps.
She's taken off her shoes, and I remember how the morning dew numbed her feet that had been chafed by her new shoes the previous evening.

Now she stops.
She stops to listen to the trill of an early yellowhammer.
Her focused attention and her flashing eyes tell me just how aware she is of this moment and of her own listening.
She presses her hand to her heart.
A high-heeled, white plastic sandal dangles from a crooked finger.
She lowers her hand, hastily, and her hand doesn't know what to do next. Hurt, it hangs idly in the shadow of her new cream-colored dress.

She observes herself too much, and she suffers for it.
She's desperate for approval and will forever remain famished.

BACKLIGHT

But now she picks a tall blade of melic grass and quickly turns it into a sentence: *The grass's dreams are short but deep.* She's excited by her sentence, and she sings, loud and brazen, to the grass, the songbird, and the garish yellow sky: "No, you aren't allowed to dare, you must always remember: Don't walk on the grass, and don't feed the monkeys!"
She sings with Kristiina Hautala's clear, ringing voice, and for a short, fateful moment she forgets the contours of her clumsy body.

She dances a few defiant steps on her sore feet and is discouraged.

She stands in front of me.
She looks past me because she doesn't see me.

I quickly step aside—I don't want to be judged by her relentless gaze.

She looks into the distance.
She sees the horizon, that's clear. It's roughly where the pedestrian overpass stands out against the freshly painted crosswalk in the increasingly pale early-morning light.

But that's not what she sees, because her mind is filled with images from Lucy M. Montgomery's dusky hollows, the swelling buds of wild apple trees, and nightingales forced to sing oppressively throughout the night.

And now the sun slips into its mold.
The gold haze contracts and turns ordinary.
It coils itself into the new Bismark chain around her wrist and squeezes the fashionable aquamarine gemstone around her middle finger; it's extinguished from her eyes, passes through the black velvet of her graduation cap, and is pressed onto her forehead in the shape of a self-important lyre.

She jumps over a ditch onto the road.
A lonely taxi breaks for her, then speeds off again.
A pair of drunken high-school graduates staggers past.
The girl, who has knotted the boy's tie around her arm, wishes her all the best.
She smiles in response—it almost lights up her face—and suddenly she feels tired: as heavy as lead.

She takes off her cap.
It leaves a ring around her hairsprayed tresses. Her mascara has flaked into a black veil on her cheeks.
She forces her aching feet into her tight shoes.
She's almost home, but she doesn't want to arrive in her cap because

the previous evening Father watched TV with a plastic bag on his head.
Inside was the graduation cap, the cap I didn't care about because Father never had one, even though he was the one who truly deserved it.

the temple in the morning

Those coming from eastern Helsinki are always late because none of the decision-makers have given any thought to the road.

First Kulosaari's wooden bridge was demolished. Then the Herttoniemi neighborhood was built out beyond Kulosaari's wooden villas, and when Herttoniemi's first plants took root and thrust forth their spring leaves and frosted blossoms, the cranes and excavators moved on to the other side of the road.
The forest was felled, apple trees were lifted by their roots amid their fertility rites, and the small red-, yellow-, and blue-painted villas were dealt fatal blows by front-end loaders.
Roihuvuori, known for its squat, boxlike apartment buildings, was born.
Vanha Porvoontie road meandered freely for a few miles between Herttoniemi and Roihuvuori, past industrial warehouses and substations, fields and community

gardens, all the way to Puotila.
A white, high-rise Legoland rose up in Puotila, too.

But the structural changes of the '60s pushed the city's working population even farther east, and imposing, Warsaw-style concrete bunkers rose up to swallow the masses in Kontula and Myllypuro; from the top floors, the remaining trees haphazardly clustered here and there looked like sickly patches of moss.
Puotinharju, Mellunmäki, Itäkeskus, Vuosaari, and Rastila were conceived.
And Vanha Porvoontie road, whose carrying capacity no one had considered, suffocated in the exhaust, the smell of burnt rubber, and the dispirited honking of car horns.
Mornings and evenings, Moskvitches, Minis, and IFAs snaked along the road dotted with the sallow gleam of streetlights in impatient, endless lines.

The door has a finely decorated brass handle.
There's a lock under the handle, and it snaps shut at exactly ten past nine, just as it does every morning.
A doorman in a blue uniform with tarnished metallic badges on his collar closes…

No, I'm remembering that wrong.
The uniformed doorman opened the doors at the university, when I went there eight years later.

BACKLIGHT

This doorman wears a dark-blue cardigan with elbows neatly mended using a darning mushroom, and he has a gravedigger's sad, dependable face.
He performs his duties solemnly and precisely, and he is deaf to shy knocks, stifled swears, and daring kicks on the door.

I join the wet, mute swarm of latecomers.

It's raining heavy, saltless tears.
Coats in shades of purple, brown, and black swell with rainwater. Icy rivulets stream down tartan bags, dark-blue sailor's sacks, and—those poor country bumpkins!—two loggers' backpacks.
No one uses backpacks or eats smoked-meat sandwiches anymore, except for these two unfortunate beret-wearing brothers, who sweat and slog their way up Ässärinrinne hill, sometimes in ski boots, sometimes in rubber-tipped leather boots. They speak some incomprehensible dialect and smell like shoe grease and wet wool, and they themselves don't even know if they're twins or not.

I woke up at six-thirty, endured my morning chill, and didn't answer Mother's questions of didn't I want coffee or tea or even a single sandwich for breakfast.
I pulled out my plastic hair rollers and teased my hair.
I exchanged my thick nylon stockings, on Mother's orders, for ones that don't get runs in them.
I sat in the backseat of the Moskvitch in the nervous,

mud-spattering line of traffic for an hour and fifteen minutes, and I knew I would be late again before we got as far as Kulosaari Bridge.

I begged, in vain, to be allowed to sleep on the banana crates in Kallio Market Hall's cool basement during my first class.

Father guessed math must be my first class of the day, and after I made Father understand, with a poisonous smile, that math was nothing more than plain old addition and subtraction, he proceeded to give me a boring lecture about how important math was for those who would mature into adults and, whether they wanted it yet or not, go into business.

I secretly kept my fingers in my ears during Father's lecture and pretended I was in a cool, dark basement where the smell of rotting fruit mixes with that of freshly roasted coffee.

There are small, cut-glass windows in the door, next to the brass handle.

A steep, dimly lit flight of stairs rises behind the windows into pale, yellow light.

At the top of the stairs there's a set of double doors, and I see a slow and ceaseless procession of students streaming from left to right through the glass: knee-high muddy boots, polyester skirts, and dark-gray pants with sharp creases and cuffs; hymnals, high hairdos, grave looks, and secretly painted nails.

I step away from the door.

BACKLIGHT

I don't want to talk to anyone.
The condensation that's built up inside my wool glove drips in icy drops onto my bare wrist.
A long-winded hymn breaks out behind the auditorium's closed windows.
Out on the street it sounds like muffled mumbling punctuated by the chirpy, encouraging voice of a female teacher.
But

now someone quickly flings open the window from within.
I recognize the plump hand reaching for the window hook. In fifteen minutes it will pick up a piece of white chalk and write a series of numbers with pluses, minuses, and equal signs on the board in curly flourishes.
They demand answers I don't have.

The wet, mute group stirs and crowds behind the door: soon the first student to faint will be carried out into the dim light of the hallway.
My breath fogs up the windowpane.
I wipe it clean with my sleeve and squint through it.
First I see a sweater—it's wonderful cream-colored angora!—and then a tartan skirt with limp, skinny legs sticking out underneath.

I catch my breath.

Ritva, my best and only friend so far, is lying alone on the freezing, cold floor, the victim of an indifferent ceremony.

I tug on the door's brass handle.
I know it won't open.
I realize the familiar flock of latecomers who steer clear of each other is staring at me, and I relish it.
I force a lump to well up in my throat, and the morning fog mixed with the fluid in my eyes to crystallize into a single glittering teardrop on my cheek.
I theatrically sweep it aside with the back of my hand.
But then

I see black leather high heels stop next to the angora sweater. Nylon columns rise above the heels, and blood-red nails plunge down from on high to gently—oh so gently—brush the light curls from my best friend's forehead.
Why

can't I be the unconscious victim on the stone floor? Why can't I be the one my beloved red-nailed teacher is so unbearably concerned about?
I certainly wouldn't make the mistake of opening my eyes right now, and my first act certainly wouldn't be fumbling to pull my skirt over my knees.

My friend stands up—I wouldn't do that—and my teacher protectively places her red-nailed hand on that thin, familiar shoulder.

BACKLIGHT

Why can't I be thin and pale and anemic?
Why don't I know how to faint?

Words are exchanged that I can't hear, as are smiles that don't include me.
As it is, my beloved teacher's behavior is utterly shocking this morning: she goes so far as to bend down to pick up the hymn book that's landed several yards away and hands it to the revived Ritva as if to a friend.

The beret-wearing brothers titter behind me.
Humiliated, I retreat from the door.

The fog flakes into an ordinary day.
The master of ceremonies solemnly opens the temple door in his mended cardigan.
The offended flock, smelling of wet dog and damp shoe leather, files into the dim temple. I'm one of the last.

She's on a train with a Finnish–German/German–Finnish dictionary perched on her lap.
Her Marimekko dress is the gentle orange color of a spring sunset. It has pewter buttons and lots of teeny tiny pockets.
The pockets are empty.

The stately Swiss forests flashing past the windows are reminiscent of lush parks.
It's hard for her to see them, though, because her eyes are swollen shut.
Even her legs are swollen beyond recognition, because for the past two days she's been lounging on a car ferry deck in her brand-new graduation outfit under a blazing early-summer sun.
She's sunburned and it hurts.
She fights a fear she doesn't recognize, and it's why she has an opinion about everything she sees, even about Switzerland, where the train that left Hamburg less than a day ago has taken her.

PIRKKO SAISIO

Switzerland is an old maid sitting on her ass in the middle of Europe—that's what her godfather said when he heard she had specifically applied for summer jobs there.

She wouldn't like to think so, and this is her response to the question that will soon be posed to her: *Yes, Switzerland is a very beautiful country, but Finland's nature is more* herkkä, *more delicate.*
She checks the word in her dictionary. It claims *herkkä* is *weich*, so more *herkkä* would be *weicher.*

She went to elementary school in the '50s and secondary school in the '60s.
She's learned that Finland is the most beautiful country in the world, and she's keen to use her dictionary to defend herself against the overwhelming stateliness of Switzerland's forests that loom so large behind the windows.

Finnish trees are slender—they're *kleiner*, smaller—but Finland is home to tens of thousands of lakes.
The light is different, *nicht wie hier*—it's yellow and hard. There's plenty of darkness.

She takes out, yet again, her mascara case from her purse. She casts furtive glances at her face in the small mirror.

The color of her face hasn't changed.
It's dark purple.

BACKLIGHT

An open sore oozes clear fluid at the most tender and swollen spot under her right eye.

She pages through her dictionary.

She's looking for a German equivalent to her daring sentence: *My face is flowing water like Jesus's side.*

Her situation is this:
She's a nineteen-year-old high-school graduate and she's decided to become the director of a Swiss orphanage.
She's familiarized herself with Heinrich Pestalozzi's ideas about the caretaking of orphans.
In her case, *familiarized* means she's read a saccharine article in *Reader's Digest* about Pestalozzi villages that provide orphans with a homelike environment that's more interesting than typical family life.
In addition to that, she's seen *The Sound of Music* eight times, and she identifies wholeheartedly with the blonde and airy Julie Andrews, who gets to be stepmother to seven charming children who adore her without having had to give birth herself.

She wants to be adored.
Unbeknownst to herself, she thinks (and is right) that vulnerable children must be the most faithful devotees.

She's familiar with Switzerland's tranquil, open expanses

from the helicopter view of Julie Andrews standing in a blooming meadow, opening her arms and her heart to the wondrous world around her.

And she knows Switzerland's characteristic scent: it smells a little of library dust and a lot of edelweiss and goat milk—after all, she's read *Heidi* dozens of times.

The setting sun casts a purple glow over the parks. The train has left Basel and chugs on to Bern.
Her suitcase is heavy, even though it's made of faux leather.
She borrowed it from Father, and there's a poorly scrubbed-off Stalinist Mosfilm studio logo decal on one side depicting an athletic man and an equally athletic woman defying capitalism and the wind, their hands held high.

She stands on the platform, her suitcase at her feet, and tries not be afraid.
Trains pull into the station.
The hiss of braking trains, the unceasing stream of people, and the conductors' shrill whistles encase her in a suffocating dome.

She's been traveling for three days, alone, mute, and sunburned, and she's waiting to tell the person sent to meet her, *Yes, Switzerland is a very beautiful country, but*

BACKLIGHT

Finland's nature is softer.
But no one comes.
No one looks at her expectantly, with delight.

She stands on the platform, her suitcase at her feet, and time runs from her.
She wants to sink into the silent ellipsis of time, to get away from this place and this moment that's threatening to crush her.
She stands on the platform, her suitcase at her feet, and lets the noise carry her away from this time and this place, somewhere far away.

She imagines she's at home, her first home, and she's on the windowsill.
She fits easily there, lying with her eyes closed as Mother drapes a tea towel smelling of Suno detergent over her; Mother covers her like all the other little cardamom buns waiting on the tray.
And there's more sweet bliss: the sound of a pure white snap as Mother and Father shake and then fold a clean sheet above where she lies with her eyes closed.
And there's more: she sways in a gentle, warm breeze on the verge of sleep, and she smells Työmies cigarettes, welding blowpipes, and freshly ironed collars.
She opens her eyes a crack and sees Grandpa's shoulder, and above it, the black sky curving overhead, full of small, bright stars. The stars are repeated on Grandma's shiny, polka-dot Sunday dress.
A sharp sickle moon sticks out behind Grandma's ear.

She closes her eyes again, and there's yet more sweet bliss: she sees an Arabian night, with skittish horses, and men in turbans holding limp, fair-skinned women in their arms. These are Sabine women, and while she doesn't know who they are, she does know they're about to be abducted.

The noise inside the station has died down.
A platform attendant in a strange cap with a mustache under his nose—the kind of mustache you don't see on Finnish platform attendants during Europe's year of unrest—walks indifferently past her, picking some debris from his pants.
Her suitcase remains at her feet like an old, faithful dog. She yawns heartily and refuses to recognize the hopelessness of her situation because

even though her plans are so romantic and childish she could rightly be called an incompetent person, as Father would put it, or a birdbrain, as Grandpa would say, she's armed with enough *sisu* and practical sense that she's arranged for herself to be here at this very station after a long correspondence with Swiss Salvation Army officials—all of which she's carried out in German.
And now

she grabs her suitcase with determination, and

half an hour later she's on a crowded commuter train on

her way from Bern to Münsingen.

It's the afternoon and the sun is a heavy vermilion.

Her face hurts and she furtively wipes away the clear fluid flowing from her open sore with a tissue.
The houses along the train tracks look like swollen cuckoo clocks, and seeing as she's inflicted this situation on herself, she has no choice but to like them.

A plump girl is waiting for her on the platform.
The girl extends her hand and says hello in Swiss German, and a memory from the previous winter unexpectedly springs to mind: she's at a house party, and everyone's sitting on the floor—they're definitely on the floor, because the armchairs and even the sofa have been moved out to the balcony.
Everyone's drunk, more on life than on the half bottle of lukewarm Bordeaux Blanc that's suddenly gone to their heads, causing a rapid political awakening and instilling a deep, lifelong friendship among them all.
Everyone swears in the name of Marx, Lenin, and Engels, and whoever else they can think of, that they will never, ever, grow up enough to start shaking hands with each other.

She doesn't have any other memories associated with this scene, and she can't because the only other memory is mine: a quarter of a century later I meet Timppa from that house party again, at a Christmas gathering organized by his law firm; we vigorously shake hands and even introduce ourselves because the years have ravaged us beyond recognition.

The girl is walking ahead of her, lugging her heavy suitcase. Her name is Renate, and the scent of freshly cut grass is overpowering.

She writes a sentence in her mind: *The evening cooled, and the wind brought the faraway scent of wormwood.*
She doesn't know what wormwood is, but in literature, good literature anyway, you can smell it in the evenings.

Renate trudges uphill like a mule, patient and tenacious. The curls on her neck are slick with sweat. Gray strands stand out in her black hair, even though Renate can't be older than seventeen.

The houses look like cuckoo clocks in Münsingen, too. There's no trash anywhere.
The dahlias, tiger lilies, and snapdragons all stand in perfect rows like soldiers, and there's not a single lock out of place in the freshly barbered hawthorn hedges.
But there in front of an old brick mill lies a murky pond with muddy ducks splashing in it.

It makes her feel at home, and she says so, in German: "Yes, Switzerland is a very beautiful country, but Finland's nature is more delicate."
Weicher.

BACKLIGHT

Viel weicher.

Renate turns. Her black hairline beads with sweat. "*Du rauchst?*"

Based on the intonation in Renate's hoarse voice, she understands she's been asked a question.
She turns the pages of her dictionary in her mind. Does Renate need something?
No, need is *gebrauchen*. So what is *rauchen*...

To be on the safe side, she shakes her head no and then nods.
Renate laughs.
Renate's teeth are few and far between, and she has the beginnings of a mustache on her upper lip.
Renate makes a smoking motion with her hand.
And suddenly she remembers: *rauch*—no, *rauchen*—means to smoke.
She takes a pack of Colts out of her purse, the only thing she's been left to carry.
Renate shakes her head in horror: *nicht hier*—not here.
Renate pulls her into the shade of a large oak tree.
The oak sweats in the dusty afternoon, and she does, too, as she lights the cigarettes she realizes will be her and Renate's shared secret.

The ducks quack with muddy voices.
The first squadron of insects skitters out of the murky water.

A door opens nearby and someone is asked to come inside to eat in a language she doesn't recognize as German.

The Captain himself is watering the lawn with a green plastic garden hose.
A concrete swimming pool ripples next to the lawn, and the buildings look nothing like the Swiss chalets with gabled roofs in the Pestalozzi Children's Village she saw in *Reader's Digest*.
The buildings remind her of Puotila, or the brochures advertising the Jehovah's Witnesses.
They're row houses with flat roofs, and she doesn't see grateful children at the pool or anywhere else.
But the Captain is in shorts, and hairy, masculine legs peek out from under the cuffs.
He meticulously turns off the garden hose, wipes his hands on a blue-checkered handkerchief, and neatly folds it along its ironed creases into his pocket before extending his hand to her:
"We thought you wouldn't dare show up at all."

This is followed by lots of Swiss German laughter and explanation: the Captain did go to Bern in his off-road vehicle to meet her—he was even wearing his official Salvation Army uniform—but of course he didn't venture to talk to any foreign-looking young women, because he hadn't seen any foreign-looking young women who looked inquisitive, much less lost.
After all the laughter and explanation, she's ushered inside

BACKLIGHT

one of the row houses and introduced to the Captainess, who sports a forbidding perm and an even more forbidding smile, and in that moment she doesn't dare listen to the wail of warning from her unconscious, even though

it's precisely because of the Captainess that she's had to secretly smoke a cigarette under a 100-year-old oak tree and then suck on a cough drop Renate offered her that tastes like Swiss herbs.

After she's been led to her room, which reminds her of the small rooms in a Finnish folk high-school dormitory; after she's let the water run in the shower for a suitable length of time—after all, she didn't want her expensive mascara to go to waste—
and after she's hung her wrinkled clothes in the peeling mahogany veneer wardrobe;

she gets to see the orphans.

It's cherry day for the orphans.
The summer's first cherries are ripe, and the orphans have hung them on their ears by the stems.
The Swiss orphans have thick hair—some of them even have fiery red hair like Anne of Green Gables, whom she adores—and clearly defined eyebrows.

Her own eyebrows are drawn on with mascara.
She has no eyebrows to speak of, only a few loose hairs sprinkled here and there.

Mother mourned my eyebrows, the ones I didn't have, and Aunt Ulla mourned my nails, which are round, flat, and chipped.
Mother bought castor oil from the pharmacy next to Karhupuisto Park when I was nine and religiously applied it every night for three years to where my eyebrows should have been, convinced they were indeed growing thicker.
Aunt Ulla fed me calcium tablets sometimes, and after the sauna she would push down my cuticles with her own strong, bright-red nails.
But

the orphans have proper nails and firm noses and well-defined lips and cherry-red cherries hanging from their ears, which

makes her feel colorless and clumsy at the dinner table. Dinner consists of fried pork ribs and sauteed spinach, and the firm-nosed Swiss orphans eagerly clean their plates, which

makes her miss pale and fair-haired Finnish children, whose eyes wander as they push their hot dogs in sauce from one side of the plate to the other.
Swiss children are beautiful, *sehr schön*, but Finnish children are more delicate, *viel weicher*, just like Finnish nature, now disappearing in gloomy fog as the clock strikes.

BACKLIGHT

She stands at her window.
The moon leaps into the sky from behind the beeches and poplars; she hears faint croaking from a ditch.
The angular row houses that Jehovah's Witnesses dream of dissolve into velvety darkness.
All the lights are off; only the capricious blue light of the TV screen glows from the Captain's living room.

The wormwood smells sweet, and if it's not that, then it's the fragrant butterfly orchid and the newly sprouted wheat.

The swimming pool's water glimmers in the moonlight, and

if it weren't for the unbearable tightness she feels in both cheeks, she would smile to herself because

darkness is falling on the first night of her new life.

one out of three

Everything in the temple is dark and old-fashioned and the exact opposite of Aleksis Kivi Elementary School, which is, after all, only an ordinary school and not a temple at all.
Slender milk-glass lamps, spaced at long intervals and emitting soft light, hang from the temple's ceiling.

The same lamps hang from the ceiling in Father's class photograph that was taken more than thirty years ago when Father made his failed, yearlong attempt as a temple acolyte.

The air smells of cigarettes, garlic, and mothballs when the leaders of the ceremony walk past carrying binders, exam books, and map scrolls.
Otherwise the air smells of dust, never of a school cafeteria or a dentist's office like the place I've escaped from to attend the temple.
There's lots of black, because the temple acolytes who are upperclassmen wear black suits and thin, dark ties over white shirts.

The upperclassmen wear gray coats and wide-brimmed Borsalino hats during their service, unlike the older boys where I came from.
You won't see leather jackets or wool hats in the temple.

I'm one out of three, just like all of us here.
We're often reminded that the gates of the temple only open for one out of every three students who want to come in.

I'm not worthy of my spot, just like most of us here.
Only the ones whose grades are read aloud when tests are returned are entitled to serve in the temple, a role coveted by many.

My stomach hurts every morning when I climb the stairs to the upper landing and see the dawning day pierce through the landing's stained-glass window, casting a dim reflection.
The stained-glass panel depicts men dressed in old-fashioned, hooded robes, holding strange instruments in their hands that appear to have something to do with mathematics and the natural sciences.
I don't know who the men are, and I don't recognize their instruments.
I've only recently learned what mathematics is, because the children in my family's circle of friends study numbers, animals, and plants, not mathematics, algebra, and biology like I do.

BACKLIGHT

I'm sure I'm the only one who's strayed into the temple who doesn't know what biology is.

My future opens before me as a long tunnel decorated with equations and characters in foreign languages, and I can't even dimly make out the other end.

hatred

The underclassmen call him the Caliph, and the upperclassmen address him familiarly as Lefa.

But there's no name that can capture the all-consuming hatred I feel when he walks into the classroom.

"Nazi" and "Pig" are the best I can come up with—but even they feel too tame.
They can't capture that particular aversion I feel when the sun glints on his thick-rimmed glasses and ricochets straight at me like a murderous arrow; when the spit shoots out of his mouth and turns into an avalanche of green slime that threatens to suffocate me; when every word he utters is a rock thrown at me.

I sit at my desk, palms sweating, tense as a spring, and I don't dare lift my head because I can hear his footsteps steadily advancing through the restless afternoon clatter and the stagnant, oxygen-starved air.
The door slams shut with hateful force; his familiar footsteps pass me—he's so close the hem of his plaid

coat almost touches me—and my heart convulses with loathing.

I don't lift my eyes, even though I'm supposed to stand up.

I don't want to stand up in his honor, but I don't want to stay seated either: if I'm seated when the others are standing, he'll have to intervene and punish me, and then he'll see how high the stakes are in this game we're playing, and he'll understand just how great his power is over me.

And so, only barely faking indifference, I remain half-sitting, half-standing, trapped in an awkward and idiotic position under my desk.

"Sit down."

I'm choked with rage—this person thinks he can control when I sit and stand!
And so I remain uncomfortably crouched under my desk when everyone else is seated.

I feel like a fool, and hatred washes over me in shuddering waves.

I take my time sitting down and try to yawn indifferently—but the tension clenching my jaw almost brings me to tears.

BACKLIGHT

Mustering all my strength, I dare to look my enemy right in the eye.
His forehead and cheeks glow hot, and for a moment I feel terrifyingly powerful.
But my enemy pulls himself together with amazing ease and glances at me as if I were a fly, in passing,

and she doesn't believe she's been seen, not even now; she assumes her teacher's flushed face must be an illusion.
She thinks she's as safe at her desk as the audience is in a theater, just observing, but she doesn't understand that the one who looks is always looked at in return, that the observer is the observed.

Almost forty years will pass before she learns that she was the only student for whom her now retired teacher felt such deep disgust that it bordered on hatred.
But

now it's the afternoon.
It's March, maybe, and it's 1963—it could be.
I sit at my desk in my green jumper, and I can't even vent my hatred by stoking it.
It's spun into a throbbing cocoon at my temples, into a grudge that leaves me gasping, and I'm forced to take it home with me to Puotila on the blue number 91 bus.

Hatred poisons my food with green bile, and I throw my spoon disdainfully in my bowl and thank Mother

for the meal before it's even begun.
Because Father has the exact same red and powerful hands as the Caliph!
The hand holding the ladle conceals the same crushing force as the Caliph's hand when he grabs a pointer and slams it to splinters on someone's desk.
And help! The same cruel, sarcastic arrow flashes in Father's glasses as the one that ricocheted from the podium to my desk that afternoon:
"So meat soup isn't good enough for a schoolgirl, is that it? You do the dishes then."

I rush into the entryway and painfully bang my knee on the door.
I rip my coat off its hanger, carefully open the outer door, and then slam it shut as hard as I can.
I climb the stairs two at a time to Ellu's apartment and ring the doorbell.
"Can I come in for a while?"

Ellu's mother dozes in front of the TV, her cheeks red from cleaning outdoors at construction sites; the dishes doze in the sink, and Ellu's hands doze on a damp, greasy dishrag.
Ellu throws the rag in the lukewarm water.
"Let's go to the mall."

The snow has turned to slush, and there's mud everywhere. Cranes and front-end loaders guard the sky as it darkens into an inky blue.

BACKLIGHT

The streetlights flicker on, and our faces turn pale.
We circle the shopping center twice.
Twice we look at the same shoes, all ugly, arranged on shelves, and the same mannequins smiling their dead smiles and wearing nylon wigs and practical, mustard-colored checkered housecoats draped over their sticklike plaster frames.
And twice we look at the photographs posted in the windows of the *Helsingin Sanomat* newspaper's local branch office:
Esko Salminen rides a motorcycle in a leather jacket in *The Gang*, which was called *Take Me While I'm Young* before the Finnish Board of Film Classification intervened.
Egyptian President Gamal Abdel Nasser has gone on a visit somewhere.
There's a new dance called the twist, and people are eagerly awaiting its arrival in Finland. The photograph shows three couples contorted in strange poses.
"Fucking morons," Ellu says.
In Ottawa, there's a two-year-old boy who smokes a pack-and-a-half of Chesterfields a day. In the photograph the boy's sitting in a stroller in a Mickey Mouse T-shirt. A large hand holds the cigarette to the boy's mouth as smoke trails from his nose.

The shopping center remains empty. We walk down Klaavuntie road toward Puotila Manor and the granary.

It's windy.
I'm freezing and my hatred won't let up.

Klaavuntie road is just as deserted and windy. A truck returning from an overtime shift splashes mud on us.
"Fuck," Ellu says.
I don't say anything.
The windows along Klaavuntie flash like lightning. Everyone is watching TV after dinner.

We won't go to the dog's grave at the manor tonight; it's too windy.
Besides, a retarded girl was raped in the woods last week.

There's an orphanage across the street.
It's an odd orphanage because it's located on the second floor of an ordinary apartment building.
The curtains have been left open, and the ventilation window is ajar.
The children are in the middle of their evening prayers.
They're singing hymns by a piano in a completely normal living room.
The light in the orphanage is yellow, even though it's blue at this time of evening everywhere else.
It enrages us.
Ellu thrusts her wool mittens between her teeth and digs a rock out of the slush; she hands it to me.
"Dare you!"
I think to myself that if the rock hits the window and breaks it, it will cause quite a stir. And a fast child could very well catch us since there's no one else on the street but us, Ellu and me, and I don't feel like running into the rape-woods.

BACKLIGHT

I find a clod of mud in the slush—it even has pale grass from the previous fall still stuck to it—and throw it.
It lands right in the middle of the window.
The singing doesn't stop, but a child's chubby hand pulls the curtains closed.
Ellu throws a rock.
She misses, hitting the neighboring apartment's window sill. The window opens and a head with tousled hair emerges.
"*Perkele!*" the man curses.
He squints and sees us. His head disappears, and a few seconds later the light goes on in the stairwell.
"He can't catch us," Ellu whispers.
We run into the woods, all the way to the dog's grave.

The dog's grave is an impressive, moss-covered stone pillar that the owner of Puotila Manor erected at some point in memory of his beloved dog.

We like this owner—we like dogs.
Neither of us will ever get our own dog since they aren't the most convenient animals for lethargic, late risers like me and Ellu.

Tepsi doesn't have her own grave, so I imagine the pillar is a memorial to her whenever I visit the grave on my own. Tepsi was put down when Grandma died and Grandpa moved in with us, and I lost my own room before I'd even gotten it.

Icy water drips from the spruce trees' branches onto the dog's grave; it's wet and shiny and covered in brown needles.

We make our way slowly down the path to the granary.
The forest rustles maliciously and I'm freezing.
I thrust my chin into the collar of my wool sweater.
I don't want to walk in front of Ellu, because I know that before long she'd knock me down or throw rocks at me or reach over my shoulder and poke me in the cheek with a long stick.
Ellu doesn't want to walk in front of me because she knows I wouldn't be able to resist knocking her down or throwing a rock at her or poking her cheek with a long stick either.
So we walk awkwardly side by side on the narrow path, shoving and tripping each other, and we're startled by the black grouse that flushes at our feet then flies into the shadows of the trees.

You can enter the granary through a window in the basement.
It smells of old hay, soil, and mold.
It was built with large, natural rocks. The mortar is covered in moss, and light comes in through the splintered roof,
and

five years later, after the granary is transformed into Puotila's chapel, she'll no longer be able to summon the same violent trembling and fear of God, even when she's on her knees at the altar to receive holy communion, to Father's annoyance and her own sweet satisfaction,

that she can now, standing in the green-tinged darkness surrounded by broken glass and cigarette butts.
"Dare you!"

I was afraid Ellu would say that.

I have to because I didn't throw a rock at the orphanage's window.

I climb the rotted wood ladder up to the loft. The loft has collapsed, but one plank is still in place.
I step onto it and look down. It's about twelve feet to the glass-strewn floor below.
I feel like vomiting.
I quickly step back.
"I knew it!" I hear from below.
I step on the plank again and half-run, half-walk along its length and back.
My heart is pounding so hard I can feel it in my ears.
My palms are slick with sweat, and it's hard to climb down because my legs have gone numb.
"That doesn't prove anything."

I see Ellu leaning against a damp stone wall in the dim light, and the rage that's been throbbing at her temples and under her skin all day bursts through the dam, so

I knock Ellu to the floor and kick her in the ribs with all my strength; I spit on her, panting.
"Moron," Ellu sniggers, calmly wiping the spit from her cheek. "You're a total nutcase."

Even Rantakartanontie road is empty and black.
Ellu doesn't say anything about what happened; neither do I.

We don't talk much. It's mainly:

"I dare you!"
And if the other doesn't dare:
"I knew it!"
And if they do:
"That's nothing."

"Dare you!"
That's me.
There's a bedroom window open at 2 Rantakartanontie.
Ellu looks for something to help extend her reach; she doesn't find anything, but I do.
It's a splintered broom handle a street sweeper has left behind.
I hand it to Ellu.
Ellu tiptoes along the wall, thrusts the handle through the window, and moves it sideways, back and forth.

BACKLIGHT

There's the sound of a flowerpot shattering. Ellu throws the handle through the window, and we run past the local Eho Bakery into the yard of 4 Rantakartanontie and on between the sandbox and the swings to the garages.
"That's nothing," I wheeze.

There's no one around the garages either.
Irma's mother comes out to empty the trash.
We curtsy, Ellu and I, and we snicker as soon as Irma's mother turns her back.
Ellu:
"What a moron."
And I say:
"Yeah, a real asshole."

The number 91 bus appears and stops at the end of the road, and things start to happen, finally.
A girl with a long braid and a violin case gets off the bus. She lives in building E on the second floor.
"Moron," Ellu observes.

The girl's father is a traffic cop, which is why we hate him and his daughter too.

We step back behind a garage and let the girl walk past, undisturbed, and then we start following her.
She can clearly hear our footsteps, but she doesn't dare turn her head. Instead she quickens her pace. So do we.
My nose gets wet inside, from rage and excitement.
Ellu grabs the girl's braid; she whimpers softly.

"What are you so afraid of, moron?"
That's Ellu, who plants herself in front of the girl, forcing her to stop.
"Nothing," the girl squeaks. Ellu smiles.

Ellu rarely smiles. Ellu's smile is crooked and frightening. I wouldn't want Ellu to smile at me like that.

The girl squeezes her violin case in her arms and tries to pass Ellu.
Ellu sticks out her foot, and now it's time for me to do something.
I don't dare touch the violin case since violins are valuable, apparently, and breaking a violin that belongs to a policeman's daughter could get us into big trouble.
For lack of a better option, I grab the girl's braid and yank her head back.
"Nice to have a dad who's a pig, huh?"
It's a pretty embarrassing sentence, and suddenly I'm fed up with it all.
"Let her go."
Ellu glances at me in surprise and then kicks the girl in the stomach.
"Just this once."
The girl runs away and doesn't look back until she gets to the trashcans at 2 Rantakartanontie.
"I'm telling my dad!"
"No she won't," Ellu says, yawning.
I'm tired too, and fed up.

BACKLIGHT

I'm fed up because now I can't show my face around 2 Rantakartanontie for at least a week, at least not alone.

Mother has washed the dishes.
I notice this as I carefully open the refrigerator to take out the hardened butter.
I guess what Father will say before he says it:
"Real food isn't good enough for this schoolgirl, but she sure can gobble up sandwiches all night long."
The voice comes from the blue living room, from under the theme music to *The Untouchables*, and I guess what the response will be, too:
"Would you just let her eat."
That's Mother.
I'm afraid of the third line, but here it comes:
"Well it's no wonder she's getting fat. I wouldn't say anything otherwise."
And the fourth line is just as predictable:
"All right then. I think I'll go lie down now."
That's Grandpa. He doesn't want to get involved in any family arguments because he no longer has a family.

Grandpa clatters about in the bathroom. His dentures clink in the water glass, and they remain there under the mirror all night long to repulse me.

Mother and Father sit in front of the TV with wet hair; I've forgotten it's sauna night.

A plastic bag filled with hair rollers sits next to the serving platter on the coffee table.

Mother hands me a comb.

"Would you put some in the back there for me, since I can't reach that far?"

"You didn't even go in the sauna," Father remarks. "You should stop all that gallivanting about during the school week."

"Whatever," I say as I try to curl Mother's short hair around a roller that's too big for it.

And I can guess the response:

"It's easy to say *whatever* to everything when all that's required of you is to put a little effort into your schoolwork, but nothing's coming of that either."

I push a pick through a roller and wonder what position Mother can possibly sleep in now.

I don't dare look in Father's direction, as I've made a horrifying observation.

When Father's hair is wet, it sticks out from his temples exactly the same way the Caliph's does.

The streetlight shines down on the Asko sofa bed I'm forced to sleep on because Grandpa's moved into the room that was promised to me.

The living room reeks of smoke, even though Mother emptied Father's ashtray in the toilet, flushing it three times before the soaked cigarette butts were willing to sink into the whirlpool.

BACKLIGHT

It's a familiar situation—it repeats itself every day. It goes like this:

I get my usual afternoon headache from the stuffy classroom and my pent-up hatred for the Caliph and Puotila and Father and my growing breasts.

I endure it by lying down on the sofa and reading *Anne of Green Gables*, but I get bored because I know it by heart; I exchange it for the first volume of *Under the North Star* and again get bored because I know this by heart too.

I doze off and pay no attention when the front door opens the first time: Grandpa's home from his welding job at Solifer, and he washes up before taking a nap in the room that's supposed to be mine.

When the door opens the second time, I force myself to wake up and prop my Swedish textbook, *Lär dig svenska*, on my stomach right in front of my nose, answering the question Mother and Father haven't asked:

"Just doing some studying."

And while Mother makes sausage soup and Father adds up the day's earnings out loud—which is infuriating—I retreat with *Lär dig svenska* to the bedroom I typically share with my parents to doze some more; later I get angry at the dinner table and then go out with Ellu and then watch some TV and then ask for permission to sleep in the living room because I have a Swedish test tomorrow.

After Mother puts clean sheets on the Asko sofa bed and turns off the ceiling light and switches on the floor lamp, I read *Anne of Green Gables* again and get bored and exchange it for *Under the North Star* and get bored again; I turn off the light, and with my eyes burning from exhaustion, I drift through the endless expanse of my hatred.

Mother carefully opens the bedroom door and walks over to the floor lamp in her pajamas, her eyes swollen with sleep.
I try to close my eyes quick, but it's too late.
"You're still awake?"
I try to whimper something sleepily, but Mother sits down on the edge of the sofa and rubs my tensed leg through the blanket.
"Is this something we need to take seriously?"
I keep my eyes closed and pretend to yawn heartily, but Mother is persistent.
"You're trying so hard, but it doesn't seem like it's doing any good."
I turn away onto my side.
I feel my pores opening in my armpits and along my hairline, but Mother still doesn't give up.
"There are other options besides secondary school. There's trade school, work, and all kinds of other possibilities."
I squeeze my eyes shut and try to force back my hot tears, but it's no use.
A tear forces its way out from under my eyelid, and to my embarrassment, it comes to rest on the tip of my nose.
And Mother:

"It's nothing to cry about. You wouldn't be the first to realize that if you aren't cut out for learning, then you just aren't."

"Let's talk tomorrow," I sniffle, and Mother pats my thigh like I'm an old, faithful dog that's going to be put down.

And after Mother leaves,

my rage is unleashed.

The Caliph's red face swells before my eyes and pushes the coffeetable aside; it tips over the armchairs and crushes the TV and the bookshelf; the *Collected Works* of Stalin and Lenin are squashed and bleed pure blood.

I have to take revenge on the Caliph,
but

she had wait two long years for the opportunity to arise.

It happened like this:
It was spring again, maybe March, and it was raining.
It was recess, and she loitered inside the school's entrance so as not to ruin her carefully coiffed hair.
The Caliph, whom she called Lefa by this point, descended the stairs and opened his umbrella, ready to go outside to supervise the students.
She saw him and had enough time to slip out the door,

but his eyes happened to meet hers, so she couldn't flee without losing her dignity.

She froze.
Lefa approached, slowing down, giving her another chance.
She stood her ground, and Lefa had to say what Lefa had to say:
"Go outside."
And she had to say what the situation required her to say:
"Oh really? Why?"
And the obligatory response:
"Because it's recess."
She now had two options. Either: *So what?* Or: *It's raining.*
She chose the former, and Lefa no longer had any choice.
He grabbed her by the sleeve, dragged her to the door facing the schoolyard, and hissed:
"You're going out that door because I told you so."
But now

she's filled with such profound rage, fueled by her family's hatred of the upper class and her knowledge of *Under the North Star*, that she wrenches herself free from the grip of her class enemy and accidentally uses the formal language of the upper class:

"I intend to go out the other door, thank you very much."

BACKLIGHT

And

so terrible is the power of my desperation that the one I hate can only surrender:

"Use whatever goddamn door you want."
And now,

as she opens the door to the rain, which will ruin the hairdo she's so carefully styled into a rock-hard beehive, she knows she's an adult.

She's St. George, who defeated the dragon.
She's Lemminkäinen, who plowed a field of poisonous snakes.
She's the Pied Piper of Hamelin; Jack who climbed the beanstalk; the prince who hacked his way through rose bushes that had grown unchecked for 100 years.
She's Robin Hood, who defeated the Sheriff of Nottingham; she's Spartacus, the leader of Roman slaves.
She's Moses, who led the Israelites out of slavery.
She's a hair's breadth from being the great Mannerheim—she's practically Jesus Christ.
But

she's only a woman after all, a girl growing into one.
She isn't afraid of being sent to the principal's office or of being grounded or of being temporarily suspended from school.
And she isn't afraid of inflicting a wound; she's afraid

of seeing the wound.
No, that isn't what she's afraid of—she's afraid of the weakness that comes with the wound as it heals.
And

when the Caliph walks into the classroom, I quickly and humbly stand up.
I look for understanding and forgiveness in his glasses— even a single, indifferent glint directed at the third row would be enough.
I've won and lost; I've lost by winning.

It's not until the fourth morning that the fog clears, and she sees the Alps.

The Alps stand out in sharp relief, as if they've been stitched on a dazzling void using the thinnest of needles.
She sees the mountains through the kitchen window, from behind the sink, and she forgets the tea towel in her hand.
"Those are the Alps," Renate says huskily, proudly, and after looking into Renate's brown, longing eyes, she writes a quick thought in her mind:
Why aren't the Alps ever where we are?

She's been at the Salvation Army's orphanage in Münsingen for three days and three nights, and she's learned many new things:

The children look like happy orphans, but they aren't necessarily happy or orphans.

None of the children at Münsingen orphanage are orphans.

There are children whose parents didn't have the energy to listen to years of crying and whining.
"Who would?" Renate asks.
There are children who have no father at all, and it's better for them to live in a household led by a man.
"One that's *supposedly* led by a man," Renate says, though she refuses to say any more. "You'll see."
There are children who are too difficult to keep at home. There are children with a Swiss father and a foreign mother, and God and the Swiss nation won't allow them to leave the country with their mothers because Switzerland is the best place to live in the world.
"As you know," Renate adds.
There are children whose parents want to spend their summer vacation on their own, and there are children who need order and discipline in their lives.

Switzerland makes the best cheese, chocolate, and Valium in the world.

In Switzerland it's horses that eat oats, not children and poor people like in Finland.
Peas are boiled in their pods and eaten with a pat of butter. Only foreigners and crazy people eat peas fresh out of the pod—and surely even they don't do that in public.

BACKLIGHT

Sunday is a holiday in Switzerland. What about in Finland?
Do you have carrots in Finland? Switzerland does.
Switzerland has the shortest military service and the most effective army in the world.
The army can deploy within forty-eight hours, and it's needed to defend Switzerland's borders because everyone wants to live in Switzerland, including the Swiss themselves. Everyone in the Swiss army has a Swiss Army knife, which is the best pocketknife in the world; it even has a toothpick along with tweezers and a nail file.

Swiss women don't have the right to vote because Swiss women don't want to.
Strange women who read foreign newspapers live in the cantons where women do have the right to vote.

Everyone envies Switzerland, and Switzerland envies no one.

Switzerland is the most beautiful country in the world, and there isn't anyone here who speaks Romansh in any way, shape, or form, even if some Finnish encyclopedia claims people do.

The Swiss live in fully finished homes and don't wander from place to place with their tents and reindeer like the Finns do.
Swiss textbooks don't lie.

The sweet and strange-tasting paste that people eat straight out of plastic containers is called yogurt.
There are even different flavors: strawberry, blueberry, and banana.

People put a butterlike fat on bread and spread jam on top for breakfast.
Cheese and salami are reserved for the evenings.

Children go to school even in the summer.

Smoking is bad but not awfully bad.
In Münsingen's only bar you can drink one glass of Appenzeller Alpenbitter, which has as much alcohol in it as a Carillo, and that isn't so awfully bad either.
What's really bad is having hickeys on your neck, and that's almost as bad as being caught alone with a boy, whether he's someone your family knows or not.
Dorre, the Captain's daughter, was caught that way—Renate knows so.

Unlike Finland, Switzerland isn't a socialist country; it's an independent country.
The Swiss speak their own independent language, which is Swiss German, and not some dialect of Russian like the Finns do.
Swiss textbooks don't lie.

In Switzerland, people shake hands in the mornings and ask, "Did you sleep well?"

BACKLIGHT

The proper response is to say "yes" and not to start talking about any dreams you may have had the previous night.

People don't sleep well at the orphanage.

She wakes up to strange sounds three nights in a row.
The first two nights she thought it was the wind howling in the eaves, and it's not until the third night that she's willing to get up and look at the moon as it illuminates the quiet valley and the robust fields full of big ears of wheat.
The moon glimmers on the motionless membrane of water in the pool and hides in the branches of a poplar, but a moaning sound persists.
She tiptoes into the hallway.
The sound is coming from downstairs; she descends the stairs and stops.

Tante Dolores, who is Tante Irma's best friend, is dragging four-year-old Daniel by the sleeve back into the children's dormitory. A long-winded cry like the moaning whistle of a steam locomotive is coming from Daniel's mouth, and Tante Dolores tries to stifle it with a white cloth that looks like a diaper.
Daniel's eyes are open but clearly don't see a thing.
Tante Dolores has black shadows under her eyes.
Daniel's twin sister Lotte walks sleepily to the door and

only then bursts into tears.
Tante Dolores gives her a light kick with her soft slipper.
There are lots of twins in the orphanage.
Twins are particularly burdensome to their parents.

Tante Dolores notices her, even though she quickly tries to hide behind a banister.
Tante Dolores says something to her, in Swiss German, and since she doesn't understand, she responds in beautiful German:
"*Entschuldigung, bitte?*"
"Sleep. *Genau*," Tante Dolores hisses.

But the sun shines in the morning, promising a hot day and an outing past the wheat field to a hill from which you can see across the valley, all the way to the pointy spire atop the town's whitewashed church, which for some reason she calls a chapel.

She gets to carry picnic baskets in each hand; the firm-nosed children who look like orphans don't want to hold her hand since she doesn't understand them and keeps repeating the same exasperating and monotonous question:

"*Entschuldigung, bitte?*"

Tante Dolores and Tante Irma smile at her from up high on the hill.
She smiles at Tante Dolores and Tante Irma, and they

smile some more at her.
She keeps smiling until her burned cheeks start leaking clear fluid again.
She turns toward the valley and furtively tries to wipe her cheek on her sleeve.
Tante Irma carefully touches her shoulder and asks, in English, if she wouldn't mind playing with the children for a moment so that she and Tante Dolores can go see if the raspberries are ripe.
She nods eagerly, even though she didn't understand which berries Tante Irma meant.

The two Tantes leave, and the children play hide-and-seek.

A horseback rider emerges from the peanut bushes behind her and greets her with a wave of his hand.
The horse's hooves clop along the road.
The wind tries to blow ripples through the still stiff wheat in the field below.
The peanut bushes rustle, and the wild roses and butterfly orchids are fragrant.
The bells in the chapel begin their booming toll, far away, and a skittish deer runs through the field.
And

now, at this very moment, her wish is granted: she is Julie Andrews, and even though she's sitting on a rock in the shade of peanut bushes, she could get up and run ecstatically down the hill to the chapel if she wanted.

She's surrounded by healthy children with ruddy cheeks and strong features, and even if the children don't worship her yet, she has time and patience on her side, just like Julie Andrews did.
She would love to gather the children around her and teach them to sing "Doe, a deer, a female deer; ray, a drop of golden sun…" And she decides she will one day.
Under her feet is the ground she's only ever seen from a helicopter's perspective, and with her own nose she can take in the smells she's had to imagine in the movie theater.

It starts to rain far off on the horizon. It looks like a blue-gray veil swaying in the wind.
The chapel's bells have gone silent, and the rider has disappeared into the woods behind the orphanage.
The children distractedly play hide-and-seek.
A gust of wind flattens the peanut bushes, the sun moves behind a cloud, and the Tantes linger on their raspberry journey.

Lightning strikes over the wheat field like a lit-up vein. There's no thunder, but a lone, heavy raindrop falls on the rock she's sitting on.

The children play erratically, and the Tantes still don't come.

Far off, where the rippling curtain of rain approaches, a rainbow appears.

The children stop to look at it and then at her, a questioning look in their eyes.

There's no sign of the Tantes, and since she doesn't know what else to do, she smiles.

She points a finger at the rainbow, which is already melting into a thundercloud, and tries to remember how to say *rainbow* in German.

Since she can't remember the word, she says:

"*Schön.*" Beautiful.

The children stare at her, not at her finger or the rainbow, but still she tries.

"*Sehr schön, nicht wahr?*"

It doesn't help.

Thunder rolls, and the children stand motionless, like Pompeiians frozen in lava.

"*Aber wo sind die Tanten?*" she asks briskly, as if the thought has just occurred to her.

"The ladies went to kiss," Miklos says in English.

Miklos's mother is Hungarian, and although he hasn't been going to school because of a sore throat, he did have to come on the outing, since the fresh Swiss air can cure any possible illness.

She doesn't understand. She laughs incredulously, and

now the Tantes appear, red-cheeked and empty-handed.

The picnic baskets are opened quickly, and everyone gets a nutritious Swiss lunch: a slice of coarse Swiss bread topped with a bar of milk chocolate.

The children chatter in relief, and the Tantes lift the little ones in the air with uncommon ease while the clumsy foreigner with the purple face withdraws into the shadows of the peanut bushes to swallow the lump in her throat.

But that evening, just before a dinner of bacon and steamed beans, she's rewarded again.
After the Captain gives the evening's orders, whispered to him by the Captainess, their daughter Dorre, who bears a slight resemblance to Julie Andrews and is studying nursing—someone you'd never imagine finding alone with a boy, whether the family knows him or not—sits down at the piano and plays the first chords of a waltz,

which I've been unable to forget even though thirty years have passed:

Jesus, der Herr will mich brauchen
ein Sonnenstrahl zu sein,
der alle Tage hell leuchtet,
und nur für Ihn allein!
Für Jesus, für Jesus
soll ich wie Sonnenstrahl leuchten,
für Jesus, für Jesus
will ich ein Sonnenstrahl sein!

The children's voices ring clear like an extra-large von Trapp family choir, and it reminds her of the couple

BACKLIGHT

waltzing on boxes of Fazer Wiener nougat and whisks her away, far away, to a small Swiss orphanage where the children live in houses with gabled roofs and fall asleep to the melancholy sound of baaing goats and tolling brass bells; they sleep soundly and wake in the morning with ruddy cheeks and firm noses.

She's the only one who lies awake after the chapel's bells have gone silent and the goats, rustling in the hay, have lain down to sleep.

The moon rises, the fire crackles in the fireplace, and after a long, eventful day, she finally has a moment to sit down and dream of her own Captain, who is a real captain at sea and so almost always away.

jacob's struggle

I can't break away from God, ever since I sought Him out in preschool.
But God has distanced Himself from me and doesn't bother granting even my most trivial wishes.

I would like to have red hair, like Anne of Green Gables, or at least be lean and lanky from growing too fast.
But my hair grows darker day by day.
I'm stocky and my teeth don't grow together in the front like they're supposed to; instead they stick out like pieces of chewing gum when I smile.
You can hear two long whistles through the gaps in my front teeth when I say my last name out loud.

I'd like to be frail, an orphan even, or at least a changeling.
But I look too much like Mother, and even Father, to imagine that my *real* mother is in dire straits, possibly an alcoholic or a prostitute, a fate from which I'd save her of course.
In thanks, my real mother would explain who I am so I

would understand the mix-up that made me this person I don't feel I am.

I'd like to be lean and coltish like Jo in *Little Women*, but I'm not even thirteen when my godfather kisses me on the cheek and says what I never wanted to hear:

"Why, our Pirkko here's a grown woman."

I'd like to be introverted and ride horses all day long, just like Pheasant in the Jalna series.

I don't want to have a full figure.

I wish I didn't like lounging on the sofa when it's snowing outside.
I wish I didn't like eating sandwiches on French bread and reading frivolous novels, ones like *Five on a Treasure Island*, *Little Women*, and *Adventures of Huckleberry Finn*; or Fyodor Dostoevsky's *The Adolescent* and Jack London's *The Sea-Wolf*.

I'd like to be popular like the girls in the teen magazine *Ajan Sävel* who are invited to go on bike rides or watch the boys' basketball games or attend picnics and parties so much it gets on your nerves.

I'd like to be a foreigner, or blind or homeless.

I'd like to be persecuted for my talent.

BACKLIGHT

I'd like to be bad at school.
And I am—but I'd like what I am good at, my perfect ten in Finnish, to shine like a bright pearl on my report card just like the pearl in Finland's crown in "The Song of the Uusimaa People."

But I'm only an ordinary, gap-toothed schoolgirl with a Finnish teacher who gave me an eight in written expression, and my parents don't drink or even separate, except to leave the Church, which I'm too embarrassed to share with anyone.

This is my situation, and God doesn't see fit to do anything about it.

I still pray often, on my side under the covers, after the credits for *Peyton Place* or *Ironside* have rolled and the Finnish Broadcasting Company's four swans have swum slowly together and then just as slowly parted. Grandpa's been asleep in the room intended for me for over an hour already.

The morning coffee Mother made for Grandpa slumbers in its thermos on the kitchen table, the water for the plastic fountain slumbers in its hose in the living room, and Teija Sopanen smiles in a taxi on her way home after having wished the people of Finland a good night on their televisions.

And God slumbers somewhere, out of reach, and I'm

the only one awake on the dark side of the earth,

until the night I unintentionally wake up God.

I'm on the verge of sleep; my hands are clasped.
Father snores gently after having stifled his yawns and voiced his concerns about the profit margin for the Greek plums he bought from Jori Koullias, given the dark spots on their sides.
Mother changes position and, sighing heartily, swallows her thoughts of the long phone conversations to come with family members should there be any complaints about the plums.
And

that's when the unexpected imperative slips into my prayer: "Screw you, God!"

And now

God is listening, very carefully,

and even though I can't see His face, I can see His eyes.

They bore into the depths beneath my sheets, and I can't unsay what I've said.
And

much worse spews from my mouth, even though I haven't been praying out loud: "Fuck you! Perkele! You do you, see if I care! You goddamn fucking devil!"

My hands are wrenched apart, and my fingers grope the air, trying to salvage my unfinished prayer: "Forgive us our trespasses, as we…"
I'm slick with sweat, and an unknown force keeps thrusting ever more obscenities into my prayers.

I don't dare go to sleep.
And I don't know where to put my hands, because now,

at long last, God is listening to me with interest.
God

is no kind god, but a god who lies in wait for obscenities, transgressions, and mistakes that can't be forgiven.
The Isrealites, who were God's chosen people after all, are the same people God drowned at sea, in floods and torrential rains; God gave them to the Moabs and other barbarians to be dismembered; and God split open the earth and dropped mothers and daughters and other female relatives into the gaping chasm simply because the men had uttered wrong words by mistake.
Children who had just learned to walk were handed over as slaves; infants in swaddling clothes died of disease; and many withered away before they were even born.

And yet there isn't a single Israelite who would ever dream of telling God to shove it or of forcing God to look at the horrific reeking images that appear before my eyes as soon as I close them.

I'm afraid to go to sleep for years.

I clasp my hands so tightly under the covers that my fingers go numb;
I fumble for the Lord's Prayer and "Now I Lay Me Down to Sleep," the familiar, albeit poorly worded, prayers I know, and when I can't remember the words, I turn to songs: "Nearer, My God, to Thee," "A Mighty Fortress is Our God," and "Spirit of Truth."
But

the unknown force thrusts ever more horrible images before God's motionless eyes: labia torn wide open; giant piles of excrement; faintly smoking devils with green tails.

I make a one-sided pact with God: if my hands are on either side of my heart while I'm praying, God doesn't have to take me at my word.
And

so for the next few years she sleeps in an awkward position with one hand on her pillow and the other bent forcibly behind her back, which causes her to suffer from chronic back pain before she even turns fifteen.
But

BACKLIGHT

I can't stop praying, even if no one hears me and my frantic words fall into a black hole.

Because even though I haven't seen His face, I have seen His expression.

the musky man, the dazzling juggler, and the clown who vomited

Aunt Ulla has pulmonary tuberculosis, which is like communism and family arguments in the sense that no one talks about it outside our home, and not really inside it either—at least not at the dinner table.

Aunt Ulla spends the tail end of winter someplace where she's given raw eggs whisked in cognac, but no cigarettes.

She returns to us sallow, thinner, and strangely calm.

At the dinner table, she picks at her plate, even though Mother made her favorite: pasta soup with milk and sandwiches with raw ground beef and lots of onions.
And while we're still eating, Aunt Ulla gets her purse and lights a Marlboro.
"So you didn't manage to give that up," says Mother, who only smokes in secret, during working hours.
Aunt Ulla squints with pleasure and shakes her head.
"Tobacco kills bacteria. In your lungs and everywhere else. Science will prove it."

Twenty years later Aunt Ulla will die from cancer that starts in her lungs.
But that's still far off, more than twenty years, and

before then we have a conversation that makes me nervous.

Mother promised me and Aunt Ulla that we could go to Lautsia Holiday Resort for the month of July, where Finnish activists grill sausages over a campfire and sing songs with German activists who have nothing to do with concentration camps, unless they were imprisoned in one themselves.
"For their beliefs," Father clarifies. And Aunt Ulla:
"But it's awful how greedy they are with butter. I bet they'll hide it in their closets and suitcases and it'll go rancid, just like last summer."
"Food's still rationed in East Germany," Mother says, and Father:
"But there's significant growth in the manufacturing sector. And it's not East Germany, it's the German Democratic Republic: the DDR. Germany's never been divided."

As I've feared, Aunt Ulla won't go to Lautsia, even though Mother thinks good strong Häme bread and butter churned from proper cow's milk—which the good people of the DDR crave more of than they can eat—would do wonders for someone who toils away in a fusty factory.

BACKLIGHT

But Aunt Ulla shakes her head.
"I'm facing a major life change right now. The doctor told me to switch professions. This girl here is heading out to sea."

Mother and Father glance at each other, and then Mother glances at me; she knows I'm getting a lump in my throat.

"To do what?"

"I'm gonna work in the galley. As a cook."
Considering my disappointment and Aunt Ulla's tuberculosis, Mother's guffaw is inappropriate:
"But Ulla, you don't even know how to boil eggs!"
"I'll learn," Aunt Ulla says. "Libraries are full of cookbooks."

The summer opens before me as a chain of inconsolably lonely days, as I lie in my sweaty sheets for over an hour, trying to stop the unknown force from thrusting its vulgar images in God's face, until I hear Father's voice from the darkness:
"But is she really up for this?"
"Well why wouldn't she be," Mother says, and based on the defensive tone of her voice, they must be talking about me. "Besides, Eero offered his kids, and you gave them the green light right away."

I hold my breath, my hands immediately seek each

other out, and an erect penis, dripping in green oil, rises out of the darkness.

"But she didn't even participate in the gymnastics events at the sports federation's celebrations, even though she got herself that expensive outfit and had herself photographed for Elanto's store window."
"I did not!" I let slip. "You wanted that picture, not me."

The outfit was in the package Mother had wrapped, and I didn't want to try on the white shirt or the red pants, not even to make sure they fit.
But the very next day, there I sat in the red-and-white outfit in the backseat of the Moskvitch on the way to Haapaniemi sports field, where one of Father's acquaintances I hadn't met before would photograph me in different gymnastic poses against my will.
And a week later, there I was, posing in a black-and-white cardboard cutout in Elanto's store window in the Siltasaari neighborhood, even though I'd lost my spot on the team in February because I hadn't learned how to count the beats that winter.
"Let's all just go to sleep," Mother says in the darkness. "We can talk more tomorrow."
But I won't let it go.
"What am I not up for?" I press. "I mean what does Mother think I'm up for?"
And

Mother has to tell me that the Moscow Circus is

coming to town during the World Festival of Youth and Students, and that she and Father plan to sell Saisio Imported Goods during the performances.
And

Mother makes Father put me on Saisio Imported Goods' payroll so that, though I lost the opportunity to share campfire sausages with the good people of the DDR, I will get to meet some of the USSR's most distinguished performers.

Helsinki is filled with young people from the World Federation of Democratic Youth.
During the day, young people march through the streets waving flags, and they dance the hopak and other folk dances by the Three Smiths statue downtown.
In the evenings, when Father and I are on our way home, we hear guitars and "The Waltz of the Partisans" wafting from the shadows under the trees.
Father hums at the wheel of the Moskvitch. Business is good, and warm, wistful memories flood his mind:
"There were so many people in Bucharest, so much singing and dancing. It was one hot summer and…oh man… Come on, girl, let's sing the youth federation's song."
And

we do:

One great vision unites us
though remote be the lands of our birth.
Foes may threaten and smite us,
still we live to bring peace on Earth.
Every country and nation,
stirs with youth's inspiration—
Young folks are singing,
happiness bringing
friendship to all the world.
Everywhere the youth are singing freedom's song,
freedom's song, freedom's song…

And Father is so moved by the song and that sweet summer night and all the others long gone that his voice breaks and his knuckles turn white on the steering wheel.
And I'm just as moved by the song and that sweet summer night I wasn't part of and the coming summer nights I will be part of that my voice breaks, too.

"Everywhere the youth are singing freedom's song," I try to go on, but my voice catches in my throat—somewhere behind the Moskvitch's windows, in the shadows under the trees, are the youth singing freedom's song, the youth I belong to but don't know how to reach.

God leaves me alone during the festival, as if He's stopped to listen closely to the songs echoing through the squares, parks, and alleyways that, to His surprise, don't even mention Him by name.

BACKLIGHT

And since God isn't tormenting me with His piercing gaze every night, the unknown force leaves me alone too, and doesn't thrust its foul images before my eyes.

I arrive at the circus early, hours before anyone else, just as Father has ordered me to:
"Target the first people in line. Go right on over to the other side of the fence, and you'll sell lots of soda and candy. No one likes standing in line, and all the dads'll buy their kids something so they'll stop their whining."

I earn a third of the evening's total earnings before the show even starts.
Father has a businessman's instincts.

I make more than the others do anyway.
I've always been bad at math, and now it's coming in handy.
I get mixed up adding together the price of two Jaffa bottles and a box of chocolate beans, and then again when I have to subtract that number from the money I've been given to arrive at what's called the change.
On the first night I accumulate almost as much change as what I make in sales.
"You can't keep that money," Erja Salme says as we stand under the stars on sawdust smelling of bear piss. "You've got to give it back."

We glance at the audience, a thousand-headed boisterous crowd dispersing to tram and bus stops.
"And who should I give it back to?" I ask with satisfaction.

The following week, when I've already earned more in change than in sales, Erja and the others decide I have to share my change with Saisio Imported Goods.

Father is in the trailer writing down our earnings for the day.
We line up in front of him and take turns giving an account of our earnings:
"Thirty-two bottles of Jaffa, fourteen bottles of Pommac, six boxes of Fasu chocolate beans, two boxes of Pectus pastilles, and three boxes of Eucalyptus pastilles."
When it's my turn, I hand over two sums to Father: my earnings and the unreturned change.
Father neatly puts my earnings in the cash box and the change in his pocket.
And on the way home, when I get to sit next to the cash box on the backseat, Father hands over the change to me.
"You earned it. I guess you're smarter than I took you for."
And

once again, the voices of the manager of Saisio Imported Goods and his clever heiress echo, singing freedom's song.

BACKLIGHT

With each passing day, I go to the circus earlier and earlier, not for the money, but to see the juggler.

His clothes sparkle, and so does his mouth, because it's full of gold teeth.

He has black, curly hair and pale gray eyes, muscular arms and a sensitive mouth—*a combination you won't find in a Finnish man* (I write in a letter to my friend Eikku).
After the juggler smiles at me twice with his sensitive mouth behind the circus tent (*shyly*, I note to Eikku); after I notice, to my surprise and embarrassment, that he gets a dimple in his sensitive cheek, and even more surprisingly, only in one; after he notices my black stare and answers it by laughing and saying something in Russian, I make a series of decisions about the rest of my life: I will learn Russian (*now I regret not having gone to the Russian language school Father suggested I attend*, I add in my letter), marry the juggler, and lose enough weight to fit into a tight, sparkling outfit so I can assist my gold-toothed husband in his performances.

I think about the juggler, all the time, more than I thought about God before this summer.
I think about the juggler so intensely I can't sleep at night.

I decide to become a communist if I have to.
And I decide to give up God if I'm asked to, or at least to

cut back on God's influence—by a considerable amount.

I think about the juggler as I loiter by the shore of Töölö Bay in the morning sun; I don't want to show up behind the tent too early, before he's there.

It's hot.
The water shimmers in the bay, and she's bothered by a smell that she associates with the juggler, though it can't come from him, because the juggler is only just getting ready for the evening's performance; he might be in the shower or having a late breakfast, or maybe he's impatiently waiting for his ride to the circus.
The smell isn't coming from the bushes already in bloom either, or from the soaked bread crusts floating in the water, or even from the duck poop.

It's a persistent, intoxicating scent.

It comes from jasmine, which she's never seen or smelled before, though she's read about it in books.
It comes from Mika Waltari's novel *The Egyptian*, the scent clinging to a woman with a name you say three times: Nefernefernefer.
It comes from Guy de Maupassant's novellas and Henri de Toulouse-Lautrec's paintings.
It comes from old, shady salons, the kinds where people lose their money, their health, and their eternal souls surrendering to it.

BACKLIGHT

She can't understand how she can possibly recognize the scent, since she's never smelled it before.

I stop.
A man passes me, and I realize he's been following me.
The scent is gone.

The man stops a short distance away; he turns and looks at me probingly.
I smile at him—I have to smell that scent again that makes me feel so at ease.

The man picks a flower—a withered reed—and holds it out to me.
The reed doesn't smell like anything.
But the man does, of something so intoxicating it makes me forget all the English I know and the juggler I'm planning to marry.

The man is from Lebanon and in the World Federation of Democratic Youth.
He's a communist, and when I simply answer "yes" as to whether I'm one too, he grabs my hand and spreads his scent over me like a veil.

And we kiss under the veil, of course we do, because that's what people have done under this veil throughout the ages.

But when he slips his hand inside my brand-new,

first-ever bra, I'm startled, and I struggle to get free of that scent's soft, seductive depths and back to the surface.

I tear myself away, even though the inexplicable scent and his black eyebrows that meet in the middle pull me back under.

And

it isn't until years later that she encounters that same scent again, at a duty-free shop in the Amsterdam airport.

She's twenty years older than the clever girl who sold soda and candy at the circus; her sense of smell has grown weaker and more demanding; and she knows musk comes from a bull's sex glands and is used, selectively, as an ingredient in some deodorants, aftershave, and perfumes.

The orchestra plays the overture to the act in which a clown pays a visit to the doctor.

Oleg Popov, the USSR's most famous clown, drinks a glass of cooking oil followed by a glass of kerosene between the bear cage and the juggler's pile of bowling pins; he adjusts his world-famous checkered hat and staggers on stage.

The clown goes to the doctor and claims he is feeling unwell.

The doctor asks the patient if he's an alcoholic.

The patient denies it the required three times, just as Peter denied Jesus.

The doctor wants to look in the patient's throat. He

BACKLIGHT

lights a three-foot-long match and asks the patient to say "Aah."
The patient breathes the kerosene he's swallowed onto the match, and out bursts a flame six feet long.

I've seen Oleg Popov's performance eighteen times. It's the best act at the circus—after the juggler's, of course.

But today, now that I've met the Lebanese man with the brows that meet in the middle; now that the reeking bear piss in the sawdust and the pig tamer's Krasnaya Moskva perfume spitefully assault my nose; now that the beribboned poodles seem depressed lying in their cages and the juggler and his gold teeth seem dull, I don't feel like selling orange soda and pastilles to an enthralled audience anymore, so I sit down on an overturned riding hurdle and watch the clown hailed as the People's Artist of the USSR vomiting the cooking oil into the gutter, his eyes watering and his shoulders shaking like those of an old man.

My earnings are the worst of the evening, and my change is in the red.
Father takes it out of my pay, and

we don't sing "The Waltz of the Partisans" or the youth federation's song in the Moskvitch on the way home.

I've paid a price for the love I've lost, but to my relief it doesn't feel like much, measured in money.

spring awakening

Mother was in the hospital.

Her absence was noticeable because no warm food appeared on the dinner table.
In the evenings, after Father came home from the store, newspapers fluttered open on the table. *Helsingin Sanomat* offered up onion sausages bought from Mantila's Butcher Shop; *Suomen Sosialidemokraatti*, smoked Baltic herring from the back of the market hall; *Kansan Uutiset*, brown bananas from our own store; and *Uusi Suomi*, meat pies from the station, which my godfather called camels' balls.

No one said anything while we ate, certainly not Mother, since she was in the hospital for a reason no one spoke aloud.
Father didn't talk to Grandpa because he'd apparently said everything there was to say about copper water pipes and welding seams in the sauna, and there wasn't anything else that interested Grandpa.

I didn't talk to Grandpa because copper pipes were of no interest to me, and I didn't talk to Father because debits, balances, and the pros and cons of shopping at different retail chains were all the same to me.
"For the time being," Father predicted.

Dishes piled up in the sink, and dust collected on the curtains and the bookshelf. No one put out clean underwear for me on the Asko sofa bed, and no one told me which shoes to wear depending on the day's weather.

A dull ache settled in the darkened corners of the living room, even though Father replaced the Airam lamp with the modern black polka-dot chandelier with five lights that Mother had chosen.

The flat rocks from Yalta turned slimy in the fountain; lines of gray scum, as many as three, formed in the bathtub; and the toothpaste ran out.
So did the shampoo and the hand soap and the flour and the shoe polish and the ironed shirts and the crackers, and finally, the Moskvitch's windshield wiper fluid, which was too much for Father:
"Perkele, this is one helluva situation we've got here."

I went to school in my gold-strapped sandals; my feet were bare because I didn't have any clean socks to wear, and the straps on my ski pants looped under the soles of my feet.
It was April, and Jussi, a classmate who later became a graphic designer, asked:

BACKLIGHT

"Did you just come back from Rome or something?"

I had no lunch in my bag, and no sugar in my blood, so I fell asleep at my desk before the afternoon.
Someone told the Checkered Soldier about my situation, and for a fleeting moment I had the opportunity to enjoy what was freely available to the bad boys every day: to stand in the doorway of the teachers' lounge furtively taking in the smell of dust and cigarette smoke and old books, coffee, and perfume that ennobled the room, and receive my beloved Finnish teacher's sweet threats:
"When a student shows no interest in learning I can only come to the regrettable conclusion that this school does not meet the student's—that is *your*—high standards, and therefore…"
Or the more direct version:
"If you're not interested in learning, I can tell you there are hundreds waiting in line behind that door who are."
Or the even more direct version:
"If you don't get your act together, I'll come up with ways to do it for you."

I wasn't listening to the words.
I was listening to the thick aroma of cigarettes, old liquor, and my teacher's poorly concealed sympathy.

Mother lay behind bars in the hospital bed in her own pajamas, thinner and straight-haired. Only the tips of her hair retained a distant memory of her perm, forming half-hearted curls.

Father arranged a bunch of withered grapes on a paper bag stamped with the Saisio Imported Goods logo.

"Eat some of these when you've got the energy. We can't offer them to customers at full price anymore."

I arranged my bare feet in my gold-strapped sandals under Mother's bed and tried to avoid the fingers that sought out my hand lying forgotten on the hospital blanket.

I hummed "The Song of the Uusimaa People" and repeated a mantra made of every swear word I knew to stop the raging rapids from surging upward, the rain from falling from the ground to the clouds, and the burning fluid from rising up my nose and into my eyes.

But

April shone through the gap in the curtains into the room, a great tit with a puffed chest pecked at the glass, and the light stretched the room into a shapeless lump when Mother said:

"There's nothing to be worried about anymore. The doctor told me I can come home next week."

And

on the way home, the Moskvitch splashed slush on families out for their Sunday walk.

"What are they loafing around in the middle of the road for," Father grumbled, and I said:

"Serves 'em right."

The first coltsfoot of spring pushed up through the

gravel on the side of the road, and the Aikamiehet male choir sent their message into the evening wind over the Moskvitch's crackling radio.
Father sprayed the windshield wiper fluid.
The fresh smell of alcohol filled the car, and Father peered out at the newly blooming landscape from the edges of the windshield.
"I guess we ought to clean up a little," Father said. "It'll be nicer to come home, for her too."
A drunk man, pulling an unwilling miniature pinscher behind him, slowly staggered across the street. Father steered the car onto the sidewalk and succeeded in splashing the man's coat and the dog's legs in a big shower of mud.
The dog yelped and jumped onto the sidewalk.
"That thing's more like a cat than a dog," Father muttered, and I said:
"I wonder if a scrawny rat like that eats cheese or the holes in 'em."

I wouldn't have told anyone about Mother being in the hospital, not even Ritva—my best and only friend so far—unless we'd been promised that Mother would come home.

Ritva is different from the others.
Ritva and I are different and alike.

Ritva has a cream-colored angora sweater, a kind I don't have, but she has gray eyes like me.

She has a curved nose and is related to many army officers, which I am not.
I have only a few relatives and a straight nose, but my nose looks like a foreigner's, just like Ritva's.

Ritva's father is an engineer, and my father is a shopkeeper and film projector repairman—but their hats are the same color and have the same deep indentations and wide brims, and they have the same way of lifting their hats straight up in greeting.

We both like Lucy M. Montgomery's books and Danny's hit "A Little Before the Tears," and we hate Annikki Tähti and politics and boys who use Brylcreem.

We hate blue sweatpants with snug cuffs, and when they fall out of fashion, we hate blue sweatpants with straight cuffs.

We love composition, and we adore the Checkered Soldier.
We hate trigonometry.
It never dawns on us what trigonometry is, even though we have it twice a week,

and I still don't know what it is.

BACKLIGHT

We love singing, but we don't learn the notes.
I learn to sing because Mother is always singing, whether it's old workers' songs or songs from where she grew up, like "Kallavesj," "The Peddler's Song," and "Savo's Song."
Ritva's mother can't sing, and we hate her because it means Ritva can't learn this thing that's an inherited ability.

But I still teach Ritva "The Varsovian."
She learns the words and especially likes the part with the red banner, and she teaches it to her mother too, even though her mother can't learn it and doesn't want to learn it because she isn't musical.
Ritva's mother starts asking questions about me, and about Father and Mother and what party we belong to and what books we have on our bookshelf.
Ritva tells me all about it, because she doesn't want to hide anything from me, and I tell Mother, because I can't and don't want to hide anything from her.
Mother forbids me from teaching Ritva or other classmates any more songs.

We're interested in the school's theater club, and when we hear that "Sleeping Beauty" has been chosen as the play for the Christmas party, we're both especially interested in the role of the princess.

Since I doubt from the very beginning that I meet the requirements to play the princess because of my dark hair, I try to get Ritva to hate the princess's role.

But Ritva has blonde, curly hair and a slender build, and the differences between us are ripped open into an all-engulfing chasm when the Checkered Soldier gives the role of Sleeping Beauty to Ritva, the only underclassman in the play.

I'm not given any role, not in the play or anything else, and from October to December I spend every Tuesday and Thursday evening crying in the bathroom, fantasizing about a future in which I'll get to act at the Finnish National Theatre in roles far more demanding than Sleeping Beauty, like George from The Famous Five.

And

the Checkered Soldier's cruelty seems to know no bounds: during the play, she forces me to sit in the back row because I'm so big.

She arranged the seating and didn't care that I'm the main character's best, if not only, friend.

I try to watch the play with disdain—it's a fairy tale after all, and that makes it a lie—but when Ritva falls into a deathlike sleep, the blue searchlight casts such a transcendent light on the profile she's inherited from her officer family that I cry out.

The Checkered Soldier glances at me from the end of the row, and even though I try to hide my shock in an absentminded yawn, there's no deceiving her.

Her black, piercing eyes bore through my sweat and

restless fidgeting, appraising me with a relentless, shameless curiosity.

Sleeping Beauty wakes up to the prince's wet, prolonged kiss, and I can't hide my revulsion from my teacher.
And the princess, drunk on the endless applause, flits off into the whirlwind of the Christmas party, so

she stands against the wall, deaf and blind to all else but the newly awakened love her beloved friend feels for the whole world, and for the first time in her life she drinks cup after cup of the black and strangely pleasurable poison known as jealousy.
And

the Checkered Soldier still doesn't spare me.
When it's time for the polonaise, which I want to dance with Ritva of course, my teacher's piercing eyes find me by the door; they expose my miserable jealousy before softening humiliatingly into pity.
Without a word, she grabs my hand with her nicotine-stained fingers and leads me onto the dance floor.
The polonaise starts, and I stumble through the steps.
Ritva keeps the tempo in front of me, nodding to the left and then to the right, her hand squeezed tight in the prince's.
The Checkered Soldier leans toward me; I smell tobacco and a foreign perfume:
"Ritva is on a roll tonight."
I nod as I try to coordinate my feet squeezed into patent

leather shoes chosen by Mother.
And she throws more water on the hot sauna stones:
"She sure is talented. She knows how to immerse herself in her role."
And

if her jealousy—which will bring her pain and pleasure throughout her life—hadn't held her in its clutches that night, she would have gone home right after the polonaise.

But she doesn't leave; instead she stares with black, empty eyes at her friend who is flushed with life and who unintentionally smiles at everyone and no one.
Ritva smiles at her, too—in passing—brushing her cheek with the slim hand of a princess, and though she notices her friend flinch, she's much too impatient to stop and think about the reason.
And it's only after

all the jostling, whispering, and laughing, when we're all together in a circle, hand in hand;
when the spruce tree that's been ripped out of the local woods begins to smell of gingerbread and longing;
when Ritva looks straight at me from the other side of the room;
when we've reached the verse where the generations have faded into oblivion in "Fair is Creation,"
that the knot I've been carrying in my heart throughout the fall is crushed.

BACKLIGHT

Now

I know there will be other polonaises, those I'll dance myself and those I'll watch from the sidelines.
And there will be those I won't be around to witness at all.

And I'm overcome with the realization that every generation fades into oblivion, and that my teacher and the prince and Ritva and I are part of the generation that's alive to sing this song now.

There were those who sang it before us, and there will be those to sing it after us, and they won't know the first thing about this jealousy that's scorching me.

This song I'm singing now will be sung without me until there's no one left, and everyone who has ever sung it will have faded into oblivion.
No one will miss it, and no one will miss those who sang it.

I want to share this revelation with Ritva, because she's the only person in the world who would understand.
But I don't have to, because Ritva looks straight at me from across the room; and though her hand is in the prince's, it doesn't matter because the prince she's been given has wide hips and doesn't understand a thing.
But

Ritva leaves the room with this wide-hipped, fictitious prince without so much as a backward glance, just like the women who trust men will help them with their coats.

I'm left alone by the oak door.
Space, which has swallowed the generations, glows black; the star-studded sky is shockingly bright, as if it's been polished.
Luckily

there's Johann Wolfgang von Goethe, who has stunned me by capturing my destiny in these lines:

Let me hold sway in my saddle!
Stay in your huts and your tents!
I will ride happily into the distance,
above my hat only the stars.

I smile wistfully.
I wish there was even one person under the stars who could see me here in my chosen solitude.
But the yard is empty.
The lights go off in the teachers' lounge.
Snowflakes shimmer on the hawthorn hedge.

I smile wistfully all through winter break.

BACKLIGHT

I even smile wistfully on the phone when Ritva tries to find out if I'm upset about something.
I pretend not to hear her questions, and I can't hear them anyway, because I'm destined to sit in my saddle for months on end with a hat on my head and only the stars above it.

All that riding causes problems when I walk, and my wistful smile strains my cheek muscles, making me look sleepy.
Father, who doesn't have any time off at all, since our store doesn't close until four on Christmas Eve, is jealous of my well-earned leisure.
"Girl, go get a rag and wake up already."

The solitude I've chosen has been noticed.

I take the rag, since getting into a petty argument doesn't suit my current mood.
Riding past the TV into the kitchen, I sit astride the kitchen table like I would a saddle and absentmindedly watch Mother, who hasn't yet been admitted to the hospital for burnout, make tarts and periodically test the rutabagas she's boiling with a fork—since they don't want to soften—and then go out to hang Grandpa's work clothes up to dry and start another load of laundry with my Dralon shirt and other dark clothes; back in the kitchen she washes the soup bowls and puts the lutefisk in the newly emptied sink to soak; she runs out to the living room to pour more coffee for Father and

Grandpa; she brings the ironing board into the kitchen and irons Father's Finland–Soviet Union Society shirt while perched awkwardly on the kitchen stool, so as to not disturb Father and Grandpa as they watch the evening news, then runs over to answer the phone.

She hangs up when she hears giggling and a teenager's voice: "What can I get you?"

The gurgling of our small plastic fountain disrupts the evening news, so Mother goes into the living room to turn it off, and while she's at it, she brings the fountain's rocks that we brought back from Yalta into the kitchen to rinse them, since they tend to get slimy in fresh water; she dries them with a tea towel and puts them back in the fountain.

"Keep it down," comes Father's voice, and Mother tiptoes back into the kitchen; she peeks in the oven where the loaves of braided cardamom bread are baking; she closes the oven door and mumbles something about them needing three more minutes; she tests the rutabagas again, which remain remarkably firm; she peels the potatoes and carrots for tomorrow's soup; she tiptoes into the living room to pour more coffee and carefully opens the door to the balcony to let out the cigarette smoke; she comes back to the kitchen and searches for the Finland–Soviet Union Society ballpoint pen at the bottom of the shopping bag and then starts making a list of the spices we're missing in the corner of a newspaper, including allspice and white pepper, until:

"Close that balcony door. It's drafty in here."

Mother closes the door and continues with her

BACKLIGHT

shopping list; she remembers the cardamom bread loaves and opens the oven door to check on them; she pulls them out, they're just a tad dark, and the voice comes again from the living room:

"Cut us some slices of that cardamom bread. I want the end piece."

"It should cool off a little first." And the living room:

"No, no, go on and cut it."

Mother cuts four slices and gives the end piece to me; she arranges the other slices on a plate with a napkin on the bottom; she brings the plate to the living room, comes back, and tests the rutabagas; she answers the phone and gets asked what she'd like now; she rinses the leek for tomorrow's soup; she hangs Father's Finland–Soviet Union Society shirt in the walk-in closet; she slips past the TV back into the kitchen where she drinks a cup of coffee standing up.

"Khrushchev's gonna speed up bilateral trade," comes the commentary from the living room.

"Is that so," Mother says as she rinses her coffee cup and adjusts the lutefisk in the sink; she pokes a fork into a boiling rutabaga and shakes her head; she wraps the braided cardamom loaves in wax paper and puts them in the bread box. And the living room:

"*Is that so*. It's not something to *is that so*. There'll be more work at Luhta, and our society will get new members."

"Well that's good," Mother says; she starts boiling water for Grandpa's morning coffee and rinses out his thermos; she takes a whiff and shakes her head; she looks for the bottle of vinegar in one of the cupboards and shakes it.

The bottle is empty and Mother throws it in the trash. The trash is full, and Mother looks for her keys in her winter coat; she kicks off her slippers and pulls on her rubber boots; she takes out the trash and tests the rutabagas again when she's back.
"You should focus on math," comes a suggestion from the living room, at a volume that's louder than the comforting voice of Kauko Saarentaus reporting that Moscow is drowning in snow, and that the problems discovered in Leningrad's heating system will be fixed shortly.
"If I only had time," Mother shouts back, and she pours boiling water over the lutefisk in the sink; she saves the lutefisk from drowning with a fork; she looks in one of the cupboards for the pans we inherited from Grandma and then gets out the grater and the stale French bread from the bread box behind the cardamom buns; she grates the old bread into breadcrumbs and then takes the butter out of the refrigerator and spreads it evenly across the bottoms of the pans; she mashes the rutabagas that are still hard, and as she looks for the cream in the fridge, the response comes from the living room:
"I didn't mean you. I meant that girl in there with you."

And as Mother mixes cream and butter into the mashed rutabagas and measures breadcrumbs into a glass, there's a third voice that joins Father's and Kauko Saarentaus's voices:

"Burbot, now that's another good fish."
That's Grandpa; he'd been dozing in the armchair during the evening news.
Mother glances at me before focusing on scattering breadcrumbs in an even layer on the bottom of the first pan.
And when there's no answer from the kitchen, Grandpa lets out a big yawn.
"If you're planning to make soup anyways."

The spring breeze scattered the clouds that had been a nuisance above Rantakartanontie road for months.
Just the right amount of liverleaf sprang up to be picked along the dog's grave at Puotila Manor.
The hospital door closed behind Mother, and the wide-hipped prince found a new princess.
A flock of cranes honked their horns as they flew over Kallio Secondary School.

The stars grew paler with each passing night.

My saddle shrank, and I started walking normally again.
The corners of my mouth resumed their normal shape, and I had the irresistible urge to confess something.

We were at the Kallio library, the rejected princess and I.
We were seated on the benches on the second floor, in

the shade of the split-leaf philodendron, from which we had a clear view of the stairs so the library security guard couldn't take us by surprise and accuse us of unauthorized loitering in a public space.

There was the quiet rifling of pages being turned, the faint banging of doors opening and closing, an outburst of laughter, and the ensuing hiss of warning.

Light filtered through the unwashed windows onto the philodendron and landed in splotches on that profile that the genes of officers—inherited from Finland's wars whose particulars I hadn't bothered to study—had refined into an angular and sophisticated form.

Ritva sat lost in thought, staring at the tips of her shoes, and I stared with rapt attention at her eyelashes as they trembled, filtering bacteria from the air.

Her nose trembled too, as did her delicate nostrils and her lips.

Ritva was a mix of Anne of Green Gables and the actress Regina Linnanheimo, the day was a mix of great promise and black shadows, and in the shade of the philodendron, whispering hoarsely, I told Ritva all this and about Mother's stay in the hospital and the God who listened to me swear and our *Collected Works* of Stalin and how Mother had taken a full day off work when we lived on Fleminginkatu to poison the bedbugs that fled into our apartment after our neighbor poisoned theirs.

BACKLIGHT

I sat on the bench, out of breath from confessing so much, and Ritva stared at the tips of her shoes.

I was naked, and I thought Ritva didn't realize it—but her eyelashes trembled again when she said:
"You're a profound thinker, Pirkko."

Profound was a new word to me, but I immediately understood what it meant.
And *Pirkko* put the seal on my profound thoughts, so

on the way home on the 91 bus, as she's hanging uncomfortably onto a pole with one hand, her bag at her feet, she realizes she's become a different person.

She's a person who has been seen.

But two days later—after having been seen has straightened her posture, wiped the sullen look from her face, and gotten her to dismiss Johann Wolfgang von Goethe as too juvenile for her—she feels a light tap on her back.

She's at her desk, too tired to take any malicious pleasure in the fact that the Caliph has just broken his sixth pointer of the semester and is trying to hide the splinters of his anger in his swollen palm.

She drops her eraser on the floor, coughs, and bends down to pick it up along with the tightly crumpled piece of paper thrown on the floor next to it.

She opens her Finnish history textbook to the section on comb ceramic vases, leans it against the back of the chair in front of her, and rips open the crumpled piece of paper.
It's so awful your mom's in the hospital. How is she? We had bedbugs too, but Dad got rid of them. I don't know how, but I can ask if you're still having problems with them. Geez, look how red the Caliph is—yuck! And hey, who's Stalin?

She neatly folds the paper and glances behind her, but Eikku, who is to become her one and only second-best friend, is pretending to focus on the 1323 Treaty of Pähkinäsaari.
Ritva is seated along the wall, under the pie chart recommending a diet of carrots, rye bread, Baltic herring, and eggs that have all turned a moldy green; her Regina Linnanheimo eyelashes aren't trembling now, because she's asleep.

Her response:
Who told you???!!!
And not caring about the Caliph, she pushes the paper onto Eikku's desk.
The answer comes after the peace negotiations in Pähkinäsaari have been concluded.
Ritva told me. Is that bad?

The hawthorn hedge first thrust out its thorns and only then dared to produce its tender leaves.
The trial takes place in the shade of the hawthorn hedge,

on the green park bench.
I'm in the middle, Eikku on my right and Ritva on my left. Eikku scrapes off the nail polish she applied a week ago, and Ritva feverishly tries to open her bag's zipper.

I don't do anything.
I sit and state the charges.

And once the witness has been heard, she's sent away: "All right then. That's all cleared up."

That's me, but it isn't me: I'm talking in Father's voice.

Eikku shrugs and picks up the bag she's had since elementary school—Eikku comes from a poor family—and slowly, far too slowly, walks away.
Now it's just the two of us: the accuser and the accused. Ritva has opened her bag's zipper and doesn't know where to put her hands. But I do: mine are folded and pressed against my sore and swollen budding breasts.

We don't say anything. We're competing with our silence.
I'm good at that.

When I lived on Fleminginkatu, I refused to speak to Tiitta for six months and thirteen days until Tiitta finally gave in and rang the doorbell, as if in passing, and asked me if I wanted to go outside and play.
I don't remember what our argument was about.

I managed to avoid talking to Ellu for more than four months after she went to Stockholm with Irma instead of me, just because I asked for two days to think it over.

I've gone five weeks without talking to Father, and Mother has gone nineteen days and three hours without speaking to me.

Ritva can't take it—I guessed as much—and she gets up, faking a yawn; she glances at me with misty eyes and leaves, thankfully, before I forget that her gloomy gaze and her head, bowed excessively low like that, are her own fault.

I remain on the bench; the traffic hums.

I remain on the bench, the traffic hums, and time slips through my fingers.
In vain I look for solace in Goethe: the snow has melted and the stars have gone out, and Goethe belongs to my previous life, a time when I hadn't been seen or betrayed.

I sit on the bench; the traffic hums
until

a note lands on my lap.

It comes from behind the hawthorn hedge.
It flies over the thorns and the newly budding leaves,

BACKLIGHT

and I have no idea

that the note that's landed on my pleated, sailor-blue skirt will turn my life—me—upside down all over again.

I let the piece of paper that threatens my loneliness and disappointment remain on my lap.

I don't touch it.

I'm positive that the one who threw it, whose eyes are the color of a November sea and carry within their gaze the defeat of Finnish army officers who intended to win, is lurking behind the hedge and waiting for me to break down.
But I don't touch it, not

until I hear the crunch of gravel and see a hunched figure cross the street and disappear behind the boulder where Kallio Secondary School students will be allowed to smoke twenty years later.

I betrayed your trust. Forgive me.

Six words and less than an ounce of lead.
One eight-hundredth of a graph-ruled notebook, the kind that are sold on Agricolankatu street during recess.
And

it takes the lightest weapons to crush the wall she's built up around herself brick by brick, month by month, year by year.

She stands in the rubble: the accuser who's forced to let go of her accusations, the deaf person who's forced to hear.
The fool who's forced to laugh, and

I do laugh as I stand up on the bench and look at my friend I've been missing for so long.

Ritva turns by the bear sculpture in Karhupuisto Park and waves at me, and when I wave back, the gesture carries the power and sorrow and forgiveness of all the movies I've ever seen.

I'm Ingrid Bergman and Humphrey Bogart and the farewell as the plane leaves Casablanca;
Margarita Volodina in her People's Commissariat leather coat and Catherine Deneuve under her umbrella;
James Dean swerving toward death in his car;
Marlene Dietrich, who can raise a single eyebrow like Ritva and Regina Linnanheimo and my daughter fifty years later;
Jean Gabin mourning his dead cat and Anna Magnani clutching the fur coat that's the reward for her betrayal;
Zbigniew Cybulski who collapses and dies at a landfill and the cigarette-smoking Simone Signoret disappointed with life.

BACKLIGHT

I wouldn't have the strength to lift my hand in a wave on my own, because everything I've built myself on has been taken away.

the purse

I don't know who Sigmund Freud is, and I don't even know his name, since I won't take psychology until high school.
That's why I have the right to plunge into shameless dreams at night.

I'm in Kaisaniemi Park.
The sun is shining and there's no wind, as is usually the case in dreams.
I'm picking flowers: the same blue pansies from my dreams on Fleminginkatu, and calla lilies, the flowers of death.
Behind the park, from the direction of the train tracks, a tank comes straight toward me, its barrel pointing at a forty-five-degree angle.
I freeze with the flowers of death in my hands.

I walk down Fleminginkatu, the street I've never really left.
There's no wind, it's a sunny day, and I'm carrying a small purse made of Napa leather and lined with the finest, spotless silk.

Strangers approach and smile at the sight of me.
Their smiles aren't friendly, and when I hear the sniggering swelling into a roaring sea behind me, I realize I'm naked.
I press my exquisite purse against my bare breasts and try to run away, but I freeze in the middle of the street.

I'm driving a car and I'm naked again.
The narrow, breezeless street meanders pleasantly through the land of the singing von Trapp family.
The car struggles up a hill to a church with a shimmering gold onion dome.
Sheep bleat as shepherd dogs dash between them, and there's even a giraffe in the flock whose neck is craned at a forty-five-degree angle as it tries to take a bite out of the onion dome.
Now I'm going downhill, and the car speeds up.
I try to step on the brakes, but there aren't any.
I close my eyes, and with the steering wheel in my lap, I hurtle down, down into a gully gaping wide open and wet.

The tunnel is wet too, and dark.
I feel my way forward with my purse in my hand. It's a shapely purse, and it's made of the finest Napa leather and lined with spotless silk.
A man approaches from one end of the tunnel; he's eating a hot dog.
It's dripping with mustard, and he wants to thrust it into my clean purse.

BACKLIGHT

I freeze in the middle of the tunnel.

I don't freeze in this dream:
I'm swimming through Europe, along the canals.
The water is warm, and the reeds standing guard on the banks are perfectly still since it's a calm and cloudy day. I'm not at all tired.
I swim through Paris, and Rome is by Paris's side.
I swim through the water of Rome, along translucent tram tracks.
The water is murky but incredibly clear, and the sluice gates and the shop doors and the stage curtains all open for me automatically; I swim through them all, never getting tired.

Renate's a bad girl.

The Captainess reveals this to me on the loveseat in the shade of the rubber plant.
Dorre plays the piano in the parlor; the black polka-dot curtains flutter in the breeze, and Miklos, listlessly dangling his legs in the pool outside, suddenly seems startled by the music.
Kurt, who returned from the army two days ago, does push-ups next to the piano, his upper body bare.
The Captain himself is on his knees in the middle of the yard.

I gather the Captain must be praying, but Lotte and Daniel are standing in front of him with their legs outstretched.
So, the Captain is teaching them how to tie their shoelaces today.

"Renate doesn't sleep well," I say in German.
The Captainess nods sympathetically and offers me

cookies on a tray.
"No thank you," I say in fluent German again.
I don't want to put my hand out under the Captainess's nose.
I smell like yellow poop and vomit that's a mixture of milk and gruel—I've just been promoted from the kitchen to work with the youngest children.
The Captainess sets the tray on the coffee table and says that no one who has a bad *something*—I don't catch the word—can sleep properly at night.

I try to guess the key word I've missed.
Was it *pillow*? You certainly can't sleep well with a bad pillow.

The Captainess looks at me pointedly.

"I hope your…"

And again there's that word!

"…is clean."

The Captainess looks stern but friendly. There must be a question hidden in her sentence.
I hope your pillow is clean. It makes no sense.
"I hope so," I try at random.

The Captainess's eyebrows shoot up.

"*Fertig!*" Kurt shouts, out of breath, and he comes over to drink a cup of tea, his upper body slick with sweat.

Kurt did 113 push-ups in one go.
The Captainess looks at her son with approval and at me with surprise.
"I must admit, I don't always understand you."

I bound up the stairs two at a time to my room.
I frantically leaf through my dictionary.
The missing word isn't *pillow* or *sheet* or *hair* but *conscience*.
I blush violently, even though I'm alone.
I have to explain myself to the Captainess and laugh as hard as I can at my misunderstanding, declaring:
"Yes, my conscience is clean."

But is it?

I've had bad thoughts about the Captain, who, lifting Lotte onto his shoulders, starts galloping around the pool like a horse.
Daniel runs by the horse, screaming and holding his hands out toward the Captain even though it was only yesterday that the Captain brutally cuffed a surprised Daniel, who hadn't even noticed he'd spilled his glass of milk.
Daniel has forgotten his humiliation. So why should it bother me?

The Captainess has gone over to the pool, and with her arms crossed she looks at the Captain in that special way women look at their sons and their childish husbands.
Dorre, who diligently bakes and plays the piano and sings in the choir and studies nursing, never kindles the same kind of warmth and playful disapproval in her mother's eyes that the Captain and the toned, muscular Kurt do.
But what's it to me?

The Tantes slap the children, tie two-year-olds to potties for hours, and eat the candy the parents bring their children on the weekends.
The children cry at night but laugh during the day.
And Lotte and Daniel and Miklos and Dorrit, René, and Adrian—they all have healthy white teeth while Tante Irma's teeth are clearly made of porcelain.

No, my conscience isn't clean.
I've already learned to hate the Captainess, who overlooks her conscientious and hard-working daughter and jealously stalks her subordinates as they hunt for crumbs of love and happiness.
I've come to despise the Captain, who gallops breathlessly around the pool to please his wife, and Tante Dolores, who lies and tells a three-year-old that a jar of jam will burn his skin if he touches it, making him afraid of an ordinary object, only to turn around and open the jar with her bare hands with no regard for the little boy's dismay.

BACKLIGHT

I hate the caregivers who sing their hymns and say their prayers but then feel fine slapping one- and two-year-olds simply because they've wet their freshly changed diapers.
And

she clings to her hatred as if it's the only doorknob she has, and by hanging on it she can at least keep the door slightly ajar to Summerhill School, to a place where children can jump on the sofas and eat whenever they want; where they're allowed to masturbate and make their own rules; where they can grow up to be free, self-respecting adults who sleep soundly through the night—whether their pillows are clean or not.

I have the evening off.
Renate is given the same evening off, which seems strange, at least to Renate.
"It's a trap," Renate says in German.
I don't understand the word for *trap*, but I don't look it up in my dictionary until the following morning, when it's already too late.

Renate and I head into town.
We walk down the same hill Renate dragged my suitcase up a month ago. The dahlias have withered in the yards of the cuckoo clock houses.
The apples blush in the shade of their leaves; people

gather plums and damsons in their baskets.
We smoke under the oak tree, out of sight.
Mosquitos whine in front of the red brick mill, in the stagnant pond among the prickly reeds, where the familiar muddy ducks quack.

We go to a bar.
The cotton batting lining the counter looks like fluffy snow.
There's a faded Alpine scene on the wall behind the bottles.
It shows a man in leather pants hoisting a Swiss flag up in the air against the backdrop of mountains.

I already know that hoisting the Swiss flag up in the Alps is a cherished Swiss hobby that requires dedicated practice.

We sit down at the counter.
The smell of roasted pork, steamed spinach, and fried potatoes wafts over from the attached restaurant.
"So good," Renate says wistfully. "But expensive."
Now I'm hungry, too.
But when

she walks into this very same establishment twenty-four years later as a published author, she has money in her pockets.
She doesn't want to eat pork, but the restaurant doesn't serve anything else.

BACKLIGHT

She tries the hunk of meat, the steamed spinach, and the potatoes fried in pork fat; she leaves her food on her plate, and feeling old and picky, she heads over to the bar.
The same fluffy snow lines the counter, and behind the bottles the same man hoists a flag up in the air, surrounded by the Alps.
She orders a glass of Appenzeller Alpenbitter, just like she did when

Renate orders us glasses of Appenzeller Alpenbitter.
It's expensive, too—one shot is a day's pay—and so we drain our glasses slowly.
It's good and has a foreign taste to it.
It warms my chest and

burns her stomach.
It causes acid reflux and tastes bad besides.
It smells just like cough syrup, and she doesn't finish her glass.

Renate is tense. She has dark circles under her eyes from long hours spent awake.
I don't ask.
Renate smokes one cigarette after another and keeps glancing around.

A synthesizer in the restaurant plays a waltz that periodically threatens to turn into a march, and waiters carry heavy steins frothing with beer.

The 400-year-old floorboards sag as the entire room lines up to dance a schottische and feet start tapping to the rhythm of the synthesizer and the vigorous vocals.
The song is about fearing and desiring a sultan's kiss.
The Delta Rhythm Boys playing over the magnetophone in the bar are no match for the synthesizer: Jericho's walls come silently tumbling down as the sultans smack their ladies on the cheek.
We're on our own in the bar, Renate and I, slowly nursing our Alpenbitters, when the door opens and in walk two leather-clad motorcyclists.
One of the boys takes off his helmet; he wipes the sweat from his brow with a sleeve and walks over to give Renate a quick peck on the cheek.
Renate flushes red, and her tired eyes light up with an oily sheen.
Renate and the boy talk in hushed tones—I can't tell what they're saying because it's in Swiss German—but the boy appraises me with his eyes then casts a quick glance back at his comrade who's still standing by the door, peering in at the dance floor with pale eyes.
The boy nods and puts his helmet back on, and Renate whispers to me, in German:
"There's a boy for you, too."

The living-room cabinet is covered with photographs of a little boy with pale, watery eyes. The boy poses in a stroller, on a potty, in a pedal car, at a school desk, on a horse, in a boat, in an armchair, and at the edge of a fountain.

BACKLIGHT

I look at the photos because I'm tired and hungry.
The boy who's been given to me is called Heinz, the same boy who's in all the photos.
Heinz puts the needle at the start of "Yellow Submarine" for the seventh time and turns up the volume again because we hear ever more rhythmic thumping coming from the bedroom where Renate and Joachim, the more handsome boy, have retreated.
Heinz turns off the light.

I smell jasmine, because the window has been left open, and aftershave, because Heinz is right behind me.

I try to focus on the photos, now only barely visible in the glow of the streetlight, but I'm distracted by the hot breath smelling of cough drops right by my ear.
Wet lips feel like a warm fish touching my neck, and I don't know if I should say something when trembling hands thrust themselves into my bra.

Renate thinks we should climb up the fire escape to the second floor, but I think we've had too much to drink: first the Appenzellers and then the bottle of white wine Heinz brought out for all four of us to share.
We decide to go in the usual way, and just like in a comic book, we take off our shoes before opening the front door.
We titter as we tiptoe up the creaking staircase, and when I see the Captainess in front of the door to my room, I burst out in uncontrolled laughter: the Captainess is the

spitting image of Flo Capp in her morning robe and curlers, her arms crossed. Only the rolling pin is missing.
But Renate screams, and slowly—ever so slowly—the Captainess places her finger on the light switch.
Light floods the hallway, and I can see that Renate is trembling violently.
"What's so funny?" the Captainess asks me in perfectly clear German.
"Nothing," I squeak—for the living, breathing Flo Capp is terrifying to behold.
"Well something was a minute ago," I'm reminded, and all I can come up with is:
"Aha."

A door is carefully opened downstairs.
In ringing Swiss German, the Captainess orders the door to be closed and everyone to mind their own business.
The door closes, and the Captainess turns her attention to Renate.
It happens quickly, in German, since it's better suited to issuing clear commands than Swiss German is:
"Go to your room."

Then it's my turn.
I try to get past the Captainess to my room, but she doesn't budge. Instead she stares fixedly at my neck, though I have no idea why.
It's

only when I'm in the shower the next morning that I

BACKLIGHT

realize I've been branded.
I gently arrange a scarf around my neck and secretly stroke the painless bruise, my first one.
I start longing for Heinz.
I forget his pale eyes and bad-tasting tongue.
Heinz gradually takes on Joachim's features, and we get married and start an orphanage where children are never spanked and everyone sleeps through the night with a clean conscience.
But

before that I'm subjected to a lecture, which the Captainess delivers in English to ensure none of the key words slip past my burning ears.
It's a proper lecture.
It has an introduction, a warm-up, a climax, and a conclusion, and everything's laid out in the right order.

The introduction:
"We are open-minded people, and we took a young girl like you into our midst, into our own home, even though none of us knew anything about you. We didn't know anything about the country you come from or its customs, which apparently deviate a great deal from what ordinary Swiss people like us are used to."

The warm-up:
"In the country you come from it appears to be normal for young girls to go out at night. We've tried to be understanding—after all, we don't know what kinds

of primitive conditions the people of the far north are forced to live in. But it also seems to be normal there for young girls who don't yet know anything about the world to have all kinds of opinions—oh my goodness how many!—and maybe it's common for these ignorant girls to share their opinions in public, in the presence of older people, to willingly engage in debates, and perhaps even to imagine that they are right to bring their strange customs to what has been an independent and civilized country for hundreds of years. We don't know anything about your country, and we may not care to know more after this experience, but if it's true that people go hungry there, as we presume is the case, then please know a hungry girl ought to eat her fill at the dinner table and not steal bread and jam from the fridge at night."

The climax:
"It's clear we've been naïve, and so we've been disappointed. We believed our welcoming home and civilized customs would change the foreigner living among us—we even prayed for it—but since that hasn't been the case, we're forced to give up this insurmountable task, though I assure you we do so with heavy hearts."

The conclusion:
"However, as we do take responsibility for our choices, we will call a good family we know in southern Switzerland who may have the time and patience to give you the upbringing that's proven too much for us.

They live on a small island, which you might find cozy. After all, you've told us there's plenty of water in your country."

There are only two pauses where I manage to interject the phrase I know from the movies:

"I'm sorry."
The first comes after the part that mentions a hungry girl stealing bread and jam in the middle of the night, which I recognize as me.
And the second slips out at the mention of Finland's primitive living conditions.
To both the answer is:
"I really hope you are."

The Captainess leaves, and suddenly I feel sorry for this old, sleep-deprived woman who only manages to keep her head up because of the power of her rage and whose bra I'm sure no one wants to slip their hands into.
I try to help her on the stairs, but she pushes me violently against the railing.

I stay up all night too, for the first time since I've been at the orphanage.
I sit on the edge of Renate's bed, pouring water against her bloodless lips to get her trembling to stop, and trying to follow her German, which periodically slips into Swiss German:
Renate is an orphan and has always lived here, and since

she's underage, the Captainess is her legal guardian. Joachim is the only person who has ever loved her, and he's promised to marry her when they're both of legal age. But if the Captainess decides to send her away, she doubts Joachim will wait because Joachim has a motorcycle and curly hair and all the girls like him.

The clock strikes six, and the sun shoots up to the horizon from behind the hill.
Renate has finally fallen asleep, and I remember that the Captainess plans to send me to some island in southern Switzerland.

I remember that even though I'm not of legal age, my legal guardian is not the Captainess, but Father, whom I suddenly miss.
I also remember that I don't have a ticket to go home until the end of August, and that my father, whom I miss, would get upset about any extra expenses and fuss, so I have no choice but to stay in Switzerland.
Then I remember that Switzerland is known for its chocolate and cuckoo clocks, and I decide to go to Bern right away to look for a chocolate factory where I'm sure I can get a job.
I pack my things, and I feel so calm, so completely at peace, that I decide to take a little nap, and

she sleeps late into the next afternoon.

Renate's room has been cleared out, and at the dinner

BACKLIGHT

table Tante Dolores whispers to her that Renate was sent to a good family in southern Switzerland, to some island apparently.

the checkered solider

My name for the red-nailed Finnish teacher I worship is the Checkered Soldier.

I have secret names for everything that's important to me.
If I used the Checkered Soldier's real name, it would be just like gaping at God.
I'd be scorched.

When I call her the Checkered Soldier—in my mind of course—interesting things happen.

First: the Checkered Soldier stops being the person she is according to her real name, her official name.
Around others, I can talk freely about the Checkered Soldier using her real name, because the Checkered Soldier has nothing to do with her official name.

Second: because she's the Checkered Soldier only to me, she is mine alone when I call her that.

Third: I can say whatever I want about the Checkered Soldier and no one can contradict me because she only exists as the Checkered Soldier to me.

The Checkered Soldier has been wounded in battle like I have, except she was wounded in a real war.
She served in Lotta Svärd, the female civil defense corps, and a bomb burned off her eyebrows and eyelashes, and sliced off a piece of her leg.
That's why the Checkered Soldier scoffs at the 1948 Finno–Soviet Treaty and the school board's rules and regulations and disparagingly calls Russians *ryssät* and communists *kommarit*.

The Checkered Soldier has a willow leaf brooch pinned to her dress and a hump like hunchbacks and brown bears do.
She has tobacco-stained teeth and thin hair that sticks straight up, and no one would deny that the Checkered Soldier is an ugly woman—except me.

Since Miss Lunova, I haven't come across another woman as beautiful and captivating as the Checkered Soldier.

When she stands at the chalkboard chopping sentences like a pathologist chops bodies, raising them up and knocking them down at will, I recognize her passion.

Sentences are my playthings, too.

BACKLIGHT

I want to learn how to place commas and periods like obstacles in a hurdle race and watch horses leap gracefully over some and shy away from the impossible ones. I want to know how to carve slices of reality on paper and crush and chop sentences, violently ripping them apart and just as violently putting them back together again.

There is no reality as such. I vaguely realized this when I was only eight years old and wrote my first sentence about reality.

Reality is the sentences I write.
Sentences can't return to their starting point without being destroyed, just like an arrow can't return to its bow and a brook can't return to the stone it's passed. (Did I just use the Checkered Soldier's real last name by accident?)
Sentences can only join forces with others like them, and they can only claim to reflect their starting point or be starting points themselves.

When the Checkered Soldier, mysterious and hunched, walks into the classroom in the dim light of the slender milk-glass lamps with a stack of essays tucked under her arm, the meaning of life is crystal clear to me.

It's anticipation.
Because

from week to week, month to month, and year to year, I wait patiently for the Checkered Soldier to uncover my secret, to look under my words, into my depths, and see my rich and broken inner world reflected through the distorted membrane of words like a sunken Atlantis covered in sediment and corals.

It's to be a long wait.
The Checkered Soldier regularly gives me eight out of ten on my essays, though sometimes she adds a plus mark. It's like giving a half-trained dog a pat on the back.

Maria has short, curly hair and wears a checkered men's shirt, which she leaves hanging over the waistband of her James jeans, just like those ryssät do.

When the ryssät heard the explosion in Vyborg, the Caliph explains, they took off so fast their shirt hems flew out of their pants, and they've left them untucked ever since.

Maria has a leather jacket and a beret with leather trim, just like the ones French soldiers wear.
Maria smokes Kent cigarettes, and pretty openly too, behind the hawthorn hedge at lunchtime.
Maria looks a lot like George from The Famous Five stories—whom I want to look like—except she's almost seventeen.

George can't ever turn seventeen, because then she'd have to sort out her relationship with Dick and with something I don't yet understand, but can already feel.

Maria stands by herself during recess, leaning against a wall reading a book. It isn't a school book. It's a slim paperback that fits in her back pocket and is therefore called a *pokkari* as she later tells me.
I inch closer and crane my neck, trying to see what it is.
"Böll," I hear from behind the book.
"Aha," I say.
Maria doesn't look up. Why would she?
I'm an underclassman.
I'm wearing a green jumper, and my hair has traces of the curlers Mother twisted into it.
I have no style.

That was the first scene.

The second scene:

The setting is the same.
The school day is over, and the small-paned oak door is closed.
I loiter in the schoolyard. I'm waiting for my parents' store to close so I can get a ride home in the Moskvitch.
Maria leans against the school wall, cutting her fingernails with a pocketknife.
I inch closer, trying to think of something to say.
"Dull," Maria says without lifting her head.

"Who is?" slips out of my mouth.
And Maria:
"The knife, stupid."
And I say:
"Aha."
Luckily the Checkered Soldier comes out the oak door just then carrying her briefcase-like handbag.
"Goodbye!" I call.
"Goodbye, goodbye," the Checkered Soldier responds, giving Maria a look that's irritated somehow, and once the Checkered Soldier is gone, Maria says:
"Idiot."

I loiter in the yard after school the next day too, even though I know Father is taking Mother straight to her sewing club after work.
There's no sign of Maria.
The Checkered Soldier walks out the oak door.
"Goodbye!" I call.
The Checkered Soldier sniffs the air:
"It's nice out today. Maybe spring is on its way."

After a week of waiting, I get my reward: I instigate the third and decisive scene.

I bump into Maria at the library.
I'm looking for Ritva. We've just had a fight, and I want to say I'm sorry to practice this newly learned skill.
But the person sitting under the split-leaf philodendron isn't Ritva, it's Maria.

BACKLIGHT

Maria's been crying; I can see it from her red, puffy eyes.
I remain standing in the philodendron's shadow.
Maria turns her head away. Now I can only see her neck and the trim on her beret and Tarjei Vesaas's novel *The Fire* on the bench beside her. And then:
"Let's go to my place."

Maria's room doesn't have wallpaper like normal people's homes do.
Or she does have wallpaper, but it's been covered in white paint. The floor is the color of red wine, and it's made of wood and not linoleum like normal people's floors are.
The lamp doesn't have a porcelain dome over the lightbulb; instead the lampshade is made entirely of paper, and it has strange little lanterns hanging from it that look as if they've been made from the thinnest parchment.
It will be

thirty years before she sees those lanterns again, in the fruit aisle at a Citymarket. They're the thin papery husks golden berries are encased in.
By then she will have painted the floors of four different apartments wine red.

In Maria's room you sit on the floor, not on the chairs or the bed, and instead of a lamp there's a candle burning in the room.
Maria's mother comes to the door to ask if I'd like some coffee or tea.

"Go away and leave us alone," Maria says.
We don't drink anything.
There's no father in Maria's family.

I start visiting Maria every day after school. I take the last bus home.
I invite Maria to visit me in Puotila.
"Oh God, you mean out in the periphery?"
I don't know what *periphery* means, but I laugh like Maria does.
I'm relieved when Maria doesn't come over and I don't have to show her the living room's imitation plush carpet, or the oil painting called *Sunset in Inari* that we bought from Hakaniemi Market, or the lean bookshelf, which isn't filled with books by Pentti Saarikoski, James Baldwin, or Albert Camus, but with a plastic replica of Sputnik, a Finnish Workers' Sports Federation pennant, and a framed photograph of Father and Juri Gagarin.
"Do you really need to be galloping over there so much?" Father asks when I come home as the credits for *The Twilight Zone* are rolling.
And Mother:
"What on earth do you get up to in all that time?"

But we don't do anything.
We sit on the floor in the dark and look at the sky above Harjutori Park.
There are as many stars up there as there are in Vasily Aksyonov's novel *Ticket to the Stars*, which Maria gives me to read.

BACKLIGHT

"It's childish. But really good."

Maria doesn't give me anything to read by Samuel Beckett or Bertolt Brecht, since Beckett writes in English and Brecht writes in German.

But Maria tells me all about Brecht, who had lovers and radical ideas about the theater.

I learn that the Aristotelian understanding of theater is passé, and that epic theater resists bourgeois values and the idea of actors fully immersing themselves in their roles.

I'm highly suspicious that my purse and my hair curlers and my incomprehensible desire to write school essays are all indicative of bourgeois values.

I don't know anything about theater except that Anton P. Chekhov's plays are over four hours long, at least if it's the production from Leningrad, which the Finland–Soviet Union Society has commissioned for the Finnish National Theater.
Father, Eero, Topi, Matti, and Antero, who all work at the Finland–Soviet Union Society, make their wives and daughters go see these Chekhov plays with their complimentary tickets.
But they come along to see the Moscow Circus, the Red Army Choir, and the Leningrad State Ballet on ice.

I also learn what pacifism is when Maria explains it to

me and shows me a round, black pin with a white crow's foot in the middle.

It's a peace symbol, and Maria pins it to her beret whenever she isn't at school.

I become a pacifist just like Maria and Bert Brecht, but I never manage to get a pin with a peace symbol on it.

I read Paavo Rintala's *The Long-Distance Patrol* and Veijo Meri's *The Manila Rope*, which Maria lends me, and refuse to do a presentation on the cod in Johan Runeberg's *The Tales of Ensign Ståhl* or the virtues of the Lotta Svärd organization when the Checkered Soldier demands it of me.

Urged by Maria, I suggest doing my presentation on Bert's *Mother Courage and Her Children*, which explores the same themes but from a pacifist perspective, and to my surprise, the Checkered Soldier agrees.

I'm a little disappointed when I realize the Checkered Soldier also thinks Bert is a good writer.

I get a perfect ten on my presentation. I'm confused.

It feels like Bert has betrayed Maria and me.

But the Checkered Soldier hasn't heard of Allen Ginsburg—so says Maria.

I haven't either, but I don't tell her that.

Maria lends me Allen Ginsburg's *Howl*, in English, but I never finish it, because now that I've met Maria, the shelf over my bed is overflowing with books.

BACKLIGHT

Maria has a recording of Ginsburg's *Howl* in Finnish on her magnetophone.
We lie on the floor in the dark, with the magnetophone between us, and take turns puffing on a burning Kent cigarette—*the taste of Kent, it satisfies best*—and Maria talks over the recording because she's already learned the entire poem by heart.

I decide to write an essay on hunger in our next Finnish class.
I write one long scream about the hunger for life, in free verse.
The Checkered Soldier gives me a nine-and-a-half.

That's like giving a pat on the back to a dog that still has a lot to learn.

"Don't copy Ginsburg, and especially not Maria," the Checkered Soldier tells me as she taps me painfully on the chest with her bright red nails. "Write in your own voice, dear girl."

I don't know where my voice comes from, but it seems to be strongest when it surges up from the yawning chasm between the Checkered Soldier and Maria, since the Checkered Soldier doesn't like Maria and Maria hates the Checkered Soldier.

Maria got a five on her essay.
This is how she ended it:

I wanted to slit my wrists with a razor, but I'd forgotten I had no hands. I heard terrifying laughter behind me.

This is how I end my next essay:
I wanted to run away, but I remembered that I had no feet. Someone laughed in front of me with a terrifying voice.
I get a six.

We discuss all sorts of things related to Jesus's crucifixion in religion class just before Easter.

I call our religion teacher Cro Magnon in my mind; he has a low forehead and yellow canines and throws chalk wildly around the room when he gets angry.

I like Cro Magnon because he sees the stories in the Bible as stories of change and growth and agrees to interpret our personality traits based on our handwriting on the chalkboard.
Elisa asks Cro Magnon to tell us the personality traits of Scorpios.
I'm insulted on Cro Magnon's behalf, and so is Cro Magnon, so much so that he throws a piece of chalk at Elisa's forehead, forcing Elisa, whose boyfriend is a Scorpio, to go see the school nurse.

Cro Magnon talks about sons who have been wronged by their fathers and winds his way from Abraham and

BACKLIGHT

Isaac to Saul and David, who was adopted by Saul but was treated unjustly just as Saul's own sons were; he unexpectedly takes a detour via Kafka and his father and brings in President Urho Kekkonen's twin sons before ending at the cross where a helpless Jesus screams his last bloodcurdling words: "My God, my God, why have you forsaken me?"

"And so the father abandons his son to die among thieves, who are themselves sons abandoned by their fathers. Calvary is the site of a triple betrayal: it's the historic betrayal of sons by their fathers," Cro Magnon says, his canines flashing,

and I remember this in our next class when we're given paper, gouache paints, and water glasses and asked to paint an Easter-themed painting.

I decide to depict the historic fatherly betrayal and paint three blind sons without arms or legs writhing above the father's smugly smiling head.

The paintings are placed along the wall, and I'm satisfied with my painting of writhing sons amid catkin bouquets and lilies and bunnies, chicks, and Easter eggs.
And the teacher singles out my work; she looks at it blankly, puts it under her arm, then disappears out the door.
"No one leaves until I come back."

Five minutes later the school nurse asks me to follow her to the principal's office.

The principal, who by his own admission looks like a rat, sits bewildered behind his desk with the art teacher on his right and the Checkered Soldier on his left.
The school nurse remains by the door, as if to make sure I can't escape.
My painting depicting the historic fatherly betrayal is on the principal's desk, and the father is smiling more smugly than I'd intended.
"This painting is the product of a sick mind," the art teacher announces.
I turn cold, then hot.

I believe her.

"So what is this supposed to represent?" the principal asks, uneasily rubbing chalk dust from the cuffs of his black blazer.
"A historic betrayal, I guess," I manage to say.
The art teacher glances at the Checkered Soldier.
The Checkered Soldier responds by staring at the barely budding hawthorn hedge through the curtains.
"And what kind of betrayal might that be?" the principal asks.
"It's that fathers always betray their sons. Like Saul and the others. Urho Kekkonen."
The principal nods and studies the painting.

BACKLIGHT

I can't read the principal's expression.

Teachers clatter about in the teachers' lounge next door. I smell coffee, and blue cigarette smoke slithers into the principal's office like a snake.
"May I ask the artist if this is a depiction of Calvary?" the principal asks.
I nod in surprise. Of course it is.
The principal turns the painting in his hands.
The Checkered Soldier stubbornly stares out the window; the school nurse picks an inconspicuous piece of string from her apron.
"So this is Calvary," the principal says. "I just wonder what poor Kekkonen has to do with Calvary."

I'm shocked, first of all because the principal has called our president "poor Kekkonen," and second of all because I suddenly can't remember who Kekkonen betrayed.

"Our religion teacher said so," I say, committing my own act of betrayal, and my art teacher, whose cheeks are growing redder by the minute, orders the school nurse to call the religion teacher into the principal's office because:

"This needs to be settled once and for all."
And before the principal has a chance to stop her, the school nurse opens the door and calls the religion teacher by his first name, which strips Cro Magnon of

his religion and the sanctity of his profession:
"Hey Risto, come here for a sec."
Through the crack in the door I see a long, hairy arm emerge from a thick cloud of cigarette smoke and give a dismissive wave.
"Hugo's asking for you," the school nurse adds.
"No, I'm not," the principal says, but Cro Magnon is already at the door with a coffee cup in one hand and a cigarette in the other.
"This girl here claims you've been saying something about a historic betrayal and Saul and even Kekkonen," the art teacher says, showing my painting to Cro Magnon. "And you're telling me this is the result?"
Cro Magnon stares at the painting, dumbfounded.
"Is that supposed to be Kekkonen? It doesn't look like him at all."
"All right, get out of here, all of you," the principal says, getting up and turning to stare out the window at the greenery in the park. "Out, out. This meeting is over."
The school nurse slips out the door and puts on rubber gloves.
The art teacher makes sure not to touch me when she walks past.

I can't seem to move. My legs are stuck in thick, invisible glue.

The principal glances at me, takes his glasses off, and rubs his eyes.

"Why don't you draw bunnies and chicks for a few more years. Do it for me if for no other reason."

Once I'm in the hallway, I feel the familiar red nails tapping my back:

"You got off easy this time, but we'll have to come back to this."

I don't dare go to Maria's after school.
I go home and keep constant watch on the phone.
I'm afraid it will ring.

Grandpa comes home from work at Solifer; he goes into the bathroom to wash up and starts singing as he shaves:
"Ripe wheat is rippling…"
It's Friday, and after Friday comes Saturday, which is the day Grandpa takes his Sunday clothes with him to Solifer so he can get coffee with his sisters Hilma and Helmi on Ensimmäinen linja street right after work and then go out dancing with Hilma's son Reino at Tenho or Sillankorva in the evening.
"Ripe wheat is rippling," Grandpa repeats. He doesn't remember any other words to the song.
"Can you keep it down!" I yell. "I'm expecting a phone call." And Grandpa:
"Ripe wheat is rippling, it's rippling. Ripe wheat is rippling…"

The phone rings at four-thirty.
It's Ritva, wondering what the Swedish homework is.
Annoyed, I tell her I don't remember.
"Maybe we should talk about our friendship," Ritva says.
I slam down the receiver and stand in the dark entryway; then I dial Ritva's number from memory and apologize.
"Apology accepted," Ritva says. "But seriously, don't you think we should talk?"
I slam down the receiver again and go into the living room and try to read *Anne of the Island* and then some Heinrich Böll, until finally I open my school Bible to a random page with my eyes closed as I ask God what to do.

"Cut away the ram's fat, the fat tail, the fat covering the internal organs, the best part of the liver, the two kidneys with the fat on them, and the right thigh, for this is the ordination ram," is God's answer.

I'm pondering how this could be applied to my situation when the phone rings again.
"Saisio," I answer, and the phone:
"What can I get you?"
I slam down the receiver.
It rings again a minute later.
"Saisio."
"Now what can I get you?"
I slam down the receiver.
It rings again thirty seconds later.
"Fuck off!" I answer, and the phone:

BACKLIGHT

"Oh! Isn't this...this should be...isn't this the Saisio residence?"

I recognize Aunt Kaisa's voice, and I lower my voice: "No."
I slam down the receiver and stand in the dark entryway, waiting for the phone to ring again.

It doesn't ring until ten minutes later.
"Hello," I answer, and there's a long silence on the line. Then:
"Is this the Saisio residence?"
It's Aunt Kaisa, who's been trying to reach us on the line, which was busy for a long time and then answered with an obscenity.

I lie that something's been wrong with the telephone lines in Puotila for the past week, and Aunt Kaisa says she remembers reading something about that in the news, it must have been in *Helsingin Sanomat* or maybe it was in *Ilta-Sanomat*—surely no one writes about these sorts of things in *Hopeapeili* or *Apu*.
Aunt Kaisa tells me she visited Grandma's grave in Malmi Cemetery and noticed that the gravestone has tipped over.
"The frost must have done it," Aunt Kaisa says.
"Frost will drive a stray piglet home," I say, reciting a Finnish proverb in my agitation.
"Excuse me?"

149

By the time it's six o'clock, the phone has rung thirteen times.
I get calls from Eikku, Maria, and Ritva—Ritva calls me as many as three times—and Father's invited to attend his cycling club's annual meeting and to give a talk in Ilomantsi about Finland and the Soviet Union's relations with the People's Republic of China; Eero calls to invite Father to try out his new sauna; Mother is invited to Kesko Corporation's marketing event and to Nepe's place for a Tupperware party; there are only two "what-can-I-get-you" calls; and Grandpa gets one call from a woman whose voice I don't recognize.

I've calmed down by eight o'clock.
I'm sure teachers go to bed early or else they're focused on grading tests under the light of a table lamp.

The phone rings five minutes past eight.
Mother answers it.
"Yes…yes, I am. Oh I see…good evening."
Mother is using her most formal Finnish, and by craning my neck from the armchair, I can see Mother quickly wiping her hands on her apron.
"Oh no, that's fine. We're still up at this hour."
It can't be Sisko or Nepe or Tuija, or Typy or Eeva or Eila Hasanen.
"Yes, yes I will. Just a moment please."
Mother carefully places the receiver on the table as if it were a treasured object; she tiptoes over to the armchair and whispers:

BACKLIGHT

"It's that ugly woman, your Finnish teacher… What does she want with you at this hour?"

The Checkered Soldier asks me to visit her, immediately.

Mother forces me to change from my green jumper into my freshly ironed purple one, to comb my hair properly, and to brush my teeth so I don't smell of onions—we just had a dinner of semolina gruel and sandwiches with raw ground beef seasoned with lots of pepper and piled with onions.
Father lends me some of his aftershave for my armpits since I don't have time to take a shower.
Mother makes Father drive me to the Etelä-Haaga neighborhood where my teacher lives, and she suggests we go by the Swedish Theater so I can buy a bouquet of carnations—they're the kind of flowers you buy for someone whose taste in flowers you don't know.
"Stop that fussing," Father and I say in one voice.

The Checkered Soldier settles in the armchair by the floor lamp and asks me to sit at her feet on a floor cushion made of different-colored strips of leather and brought home as a souvenir.

I pull down the hem of my skirt, waiting for the game to begin.

The opening move:
"Oh, would you like to try these?"

And the Checkered Soldier offers me a fruit bowl filled with apples, oranges, and a banana, with fruit knives sticking out in four different directions.

I choose an orange since there are more of them than any other fruit.

I immediately regret my choice, because it means I also have to take a fruit knife to slice into the orange's dimpled rind. Juice squirts from the cut into my eye, and the Checkered Soldier, who has settled back comfortably in her chair and turned off the lights, has to get up again, turn on the lights, and go look for a tissue in the bedroom.

I take a quick look around.

The Checkered Soldier's home is more ordinary than I'd imagined.

She does have more books on her shelves than Maria does, but she's obviously bought her sofa bed from Asko, just like we have.

She has a linoleum floor, and it's covered in the same plush carpeting we have.

Her ceiling lamp has five domes, just like the one the Koskipatos and the Lehtonens and the Kalervos and the Turunens and the Järvis and Ritva and my family have.

A daintily painted grandfather clock stands in one corner; the Checkered Soldier comes from Ostrobothnia.

A spindle that's been refashioned into a candleholder is screwed into the wall beside the grandfather clock, and I decide to buy one just like it as a Mother's Day present.

BACKLIGHT

Shriveled cacti line her windowsill. They clearly haven't been watered in months.
The Checkered Soldier doesn't have a TV like the Koskipatos, Lehtonens, Kalervos, Turunens, Järvis, Ritva, and my family do.
None of the teachers own a TV, except for one of the substitute art teachers who admitted she likes Dr. Ben Casey better than Dr. Kildare.
The teachers say there's nothing but uncivilized entertainment on TV.

The Checkered Soldier returns, turns off the lights, and sits down in her armchair under the magical light of the floor lamp.

And the Checkered Soldier begins by talking about ordinary things, like the importance of skiing, bicycling, and going out for walks; drinking milk and keeping regular mealtimes; taking vitamins and getting a good night's sleep; and the Checkered Soldier doesn't seem to realize that

her listener glides far away, out of the reach of words, surrendering herself to her teacher's even, raspy voice and the sound of gurgling radiators, the evening news carrying through the walls, and the traffic humming on the other side of the window.
The smell of the orange's freshly exposed flesh mixes with the smell of dust, the ink from the *Uusi Suomi* newspaper in the magazine rack, and, to her dismay,

something she recognizes from home: malt whiskey.

The floor lamp creates a clearly delineated circle of light in the darkness, and in that light there is little to look at: there's the dwindling flesh of the orange; the seeds she carefully hides in the folds of her tissue; her own hands, sticky and stained by the orange; and her teacher's red-nailed hands, which are themselves stained.

The hands are wrinkled, seen up close; they have a few distinct liver spots, too.
They fidget restlessly with the hem of their owner's skirt, just like the hands of people addicted to smoking do, and

she wishes they would flutter from the hem to her hair or her cheek.
She's afraid it might happen.

"So what do you say?"

The Checkered Soldier has asked me something.
I wasn't listening, and I don't know how to answer.

"Excuse me?"

I'm forced to look up.
The Checkered Soldier's penetrating black eyes look at me from above, gently and reproachingly, just as I've always hoped they would.

BACKLIGHT

And just as I've feared, I can't withstand that gaze.

I look at my own hands again, at the fleshy remains of the orange, and at the Checkered Soldier's legs and her thin spring nylons with a run that she's stopped using blood-red fingernail polish.

Her legs are Doric columns I would love to lean against.

I'm so drawn to them that I have to force myself to lean in the opposite direction.
"So let's keep this conversation confidential, just between the two of us, shall we?"

And then the Checkered Soldier starts talking about Maria, and as my teacher's breathing quickens, I realize we're approaching the heart of the matter.

Maria is a deeply disturbed girl whom the Checkered Soldier has endeavored to help in every possible way, without, unfortunately, getting any kind of response from her student, who you could say is more of a patient.
Maria dresses and acts in a pathetic manner, supposedly expressing rebellion but in reality reflecting only poor taste and poor upbringing.
Maria isn't stupid, but she's only been able to absorb the crudest and most rudimentary elements from her vast literary collection,

and the Checkered Soldier recites the following familiar lines as evidence:
I wanted to slit my wrists with a razor, but I'd forgotten I had no hands. I heard terrifying laughter behind me.

"No normal, well-balanced seventeen-year-old writes something like that," the Checkered Soldier says. "And if it's meant to show impressive literary skill, all I can say is that this is banalized Beckett, a kind of poor man's Kafka. Work like this falls flat on its own arrogant face."

And now

the Checkered Soldier's hand flies from the hem of her skirt to my head.

"I apologize for being so vulgar, but damn it all to hell if a girl like her ruins a future writer!"

The Checkered Soldier's hand presses down on my head like an iron-hot skullcap.
It's hard to breathe, and I want out from under that cap. But the hand stays on my head, and the fingers move slightly, rearranging my hair and mixing up my thoughts.

Did the Checkered Soldier say the word *writer*?
She did.
Did the Checkered Soldier mean *me*?

She did. She didn't. I don't know.

But that's exactly what I need to know.
I'm Odysseus. I've heard the call of the sirens.
"So you mean Maria could maybe become a writer if…"

I don't know how to continue my poorly disguised question.
The Checkered Soldier pulls her hand away, but the imprint of her hand continues to burn on my head.

The Checkered Soldier laughs:

"Who knows what anyone will become. But you will become a writer if…"

And the Checkered Soldier says nothing more.

The *if* hangs over my head like Damocles's sword.
The Checkered Soldier leaves it hanging there: she gets up to turn on the lights, moves a pack of Amiro cigarettes behind a cactus, and then stops by the window to stare outside.

The Checkered Soldier lets me stare at her mute back and then quickly changes the subject.

"Pathetically ordinary scribble, that Calvary painting of yours that caused such a fuss today. That's not evidence of a disturbed mind."

And the Checkered Soldier turns, thrusting an Amiro cigarette in her mouth and lighting it. She looks at me through the smoke.
"It's one hell of an insolent attempt at imitating art, that's what it is."

I'm ready to confess my insolence and my poor artistic abilities and even much worse, if only the Checkered Soldier will agree to open Pandora's box and reveal what's behind the *if* and the gift she's promised me.
And

even though she's young and confused, she isn't naïve—she knows there's a deal involved.

Her beloved's eyes scorch her in the naked light of the floor lamp, and her beloved can do what she can't: stand there motionless, hiding the gift behind her back and letting the silence grow into a suffocatingly thick plastic film that envelops the room.
She's forced to submit:
"I could be…or…"
"You could be," the Checkered Soldier helps me along.
"…a writer, if…"
"If you cut off all ties with that girl."

I go into my parents' bedroom with my coat on.
Father is already asleep, but Mother is reading *Uusi*

BACKLIGHT

Nainen magazine under the covers.
"So what did she say?"
"Who?"
Mother's irritated:
"Well your Finnish teacher of course. I'm sure she didn't make you go to Etelä-Haaga for nothing."
"She didn't make me do anything—it was an invitation."
"Nonsense," Mother says as she throws the magazine on the floor and then rearranges her pillow under her neck so her curlers won't hurt. "Come on, tell me what happened."

I hold my secret like you hold your breath.
I let it expand from my stomach and up to my chest where it swells and swells until I let it out through my mouth:
"She says I'm going to be a writer."

I'm breathless, and my voice cracks from the embarrassing sob stuck in my throat.
Father opens his eyes and sits up in bed.
He has the familiar crease on his forehead that he always gets when sleeping.
And he looks at Mother, as he almost always does when he talks to me:
"Now is it really appropriate to confuse her with that kind of nonsense?"

And for once I hear the voice under the words, and I understand the contradiction between Father's words and his tone.

Father wipes the sleep from his eyes; his eyes light up with an appraising gleam.

But Mother's eyes don't light up:

"But why was she in such a hurry to tell you tonight of all nights?"
I don't know how to answer.
Mother shoves her feet into her gold-embroidered slippers that Aunt Ulla brought back from the Canary Islands, a place where bananas are three feet long and you can have croissants and Kahlua for breakfast if you want.
"Let's go have a proper cup of coffee."

Mother wraps her dressing gown around her with purpose—she knows the Checkered Soldier and I have made a deal.

"Engineers and writers like Väinö Linna earn the same monthly salary," Father says, laying his head back on his pillow. "Engineers with a master's degree anyway."

"So you promised to stop seeing your friend, just like that," Mother says, dipping a rusk made from an Eho Bakery cinnamon roll in her coffee. "I had no idea secondary-school teachers ordered students around in their private lives, too."

"That's not what this is about," I say, feeling tired.

BACKLIGHT

The magic circle under the floor lamp, the Checkered Soldier's touch, and the idea of authorship have all been snuffed out in the insignificance of everyday life.

"So what is it about then?"
Mother torments me with her gaze, which may not be as mysterious but is every bit as penetrating as the Checkered Soldier's.
I don't have the energy to answer.
Mother's scrupulous prying is stripping me of my fate as if it were a cape that's only just been draped over my shoulders.

Mother doesn't understand that I'm naked under that cape.

"You don't understand anything," I manage to say.
"I understand what I understand," Mother says. She's clearly gearing up for a full-on argument.
"No one ever leaves me alone," I say.
"Oh is that it, no one ever leaves you alone!" Mother yells wildly. "We give you everything, food, clothes, you name it; we pay your tuition and buy your school books with our hard-earned money. We take you to school and bring you home again; you've got your own desk and your own bookshelves; you've got a school bag and pens and pencil cases, pencil extenders and desk protectors, whatever you can think to ask for. And the only thing we ask in return is that you focus a little on your schoolwork. Really it'd be easier on us if we took you out of that school and put you

behind the cash register. Maybe we should have you earn your own money and wash and iron your own clothes, then you'll see what it's like!"

I go to sleep in the living room.
Mother's griping follows the usual pattern, like a puzzle that's been solved a hundred times before, one that involves connecting the dots to reveal a picture.

I get my coat from the entryway and pull it over me.
I close my eyes.
"That's exactly how it is and exactly how it's going to be," I hear in the dark. "When a person can't even get a proper blanket to put over themselves."
The bedroom door opens, then the door to the walk-in closet, and the bedroom door closes.
A pile of sheets smelling of Omo detergent is dropped on top of me, and Mother's voice, suddenly conciliatory: "And you want to be a writer. Goodness gracious, what an idea."
"Maybe I will be," I say without opening my eyes.
"Yes indeed," Mother says, sitting down on the edge of the sofa. "But dear child, please try to understand that no one can promise you a job as a writer, though no one can take it away from you either, no matter what kind of conditions or promises or vows they might make."

And in the darkness a hand approaches my hair, which is still the way the Checkered Soldier arranged it; it stops before its target and pulls back.

BACKLIGHT

"Now put the sheets on properly, so you aren't sleeping there like some vagabond."

And after Mother leaves,

she wakes up from her prolonged anticipation.

She's shipwrecked on a shore that's deserted and dark and hers alone.
The Atlantis that's covered in sediment and corals will rise on account of her strength if it is to rise, just like it sank on account of her weakness.

The picture of her beloved fades on the horizon, and

the next day she no longer calls her teacher the Checkered Soldier, and she never calls her by that name again.

marx, electricity, and opium

Despite my fervent prayers, God refuses to show Himself to me, even though I've heard He appears to entire congregations of Jehovah's Witnesses and the Saalem Pentecostal Church at the smallest request.

Even Kristiina has seen God, in a Kingdom Hall, together with her mother and father.
"Well, what did the old man look like?" I ask provocatively.
"God is no *old man*!" Kristiina says, indignantly opening her desk lid.
"Well, what did he, with a capital *h*, look like then?" I try, but Kristiina opens her pearl-beaded Bible and focuses her attention on it, her cheeks flushed.
"So you haven't seen God!" I jeer triumphantly, and Kristiina, behind her Bible:
"God shows Himself to us through his Word, letter by letter. Focus on that and cut the crap."

Father hates God, who doesn't exist.

At the dinner table, between the pea soup and the pancakes:
"There's no such thing as God. It all started with the Big Bang, as the atheists have proven."
And during evening coffee, between a Danish pastry and his last drags on a cigarette for the night:
"God, now there's a crafty bugger for you. Been keeping poor people submissive throughout history so they won't stand up for their rights."
"But God doesn't exist," I say eagerly.
"That's right, he doesn't," Father answers with satisfaction. "Science has proven it multiple times over."
"So how can something that doesn't exist be crafty?"
Father blinks, stubs out his half-smoked cigarette, and turns his attention to *The Untouchables*.
"But how can something have any characteristics if it doesn't even exist?" I ask, gaining new momentum.
And Mother whispers:
"Let's not get him all worked up."
And Father says to Mother, not turning his head:
"They sure know how to turn 'em into smart alecks at that school. She ought to spend a little more time learning something useful and a little less nitpicking."

"So can donkeys talk?" I ask Kristiina.
She looks at me suspiciously, as you would at someone who's pointing a knife at you.
"How come?"
"Well can they?"
Kristiina thinks for a moment, glancing at her Bible,

and makes her decision:
"Of course they can't. Speech is a gift God gave only to people."
"But Balaam's donkey could!" I say triumphantly.
Kristiina glances toward the door, but when our English teacher still doesn't appear, she shrugs her shoulders.
"That must be a fairy tale."
"Of course it's a fairy tale!" I say, and my fingers tremble as I look for the page in my school Bible where Balaam's donkey scolds his hard-hearted master.
Kristiina reads the passage and then looks up at me, delighted.
"Donkeys used to be able to talk… I didn't know that!"

I hate God, who lurks in the murky maze of his writings, and I hate his lackeys, who don't even recognize the existence of gray areas.

"Religion is the opium of the people," Father says in the entryway.
Mother pretends to watch TV as she irons Grandpa's Sunday pants, but based on her clenched jaw and the jerky movement of the iron, I can tell Mother can't help but listen to the conversation taking place in the entryway.
I wink at her, but Mother pretends not to notice anything, not even me.
"What is?" a fragile voice asks.
"Oh stop it already!" Mother snaps, but Father:

"Opium."

Mother is embarrassed that Father keeps the Jehovah's Witnesses standing in the entryway without inviting them in or sending them away, and that he uses the informal *you* to address the elderly:
"Oh come on now, surely you must realize that science has freed humankind from religion and all that nonsense."

"Oh, opium," I say, after Father has pulled up his pant legs, cleared his throat for the benefit of Lenin's and Stalin's *Collected Works*, and settled in his armchair, tapping his cooled coffee, which Mother quickly rushes into the kitchen to replace.

"Marx has proven it," Father says, and I say:
"I know. But what is *opium* exactly?"
"You're the one who should know that, since you're the one getting an education," Father says, looking at Mother. "With my money."
"Oh *your* money?" Mother lets slip behind the ironing board.
After Grandpa's Sunday pants it's my green jumper's turn.
"I mean *ours*," Father corrects himself. "But still."

Mother blinks at me in warning; I barely notice it out of the corner of my eye, as I have no intention of backing down.

BACKLIGHT

"I do know what it is, but I bet you don't, even though you're always going on about it."
"Please don't start again!" Mother almost shrieks.
"If you read up on your Marx, maybe you'd finally get some common sense," says Father's profile, focused on the TV.
His hand holding the coffee cup is trembling slightly, but I can't stop myself.
"So what is Marxism exactly?"
"Marxism-Leninism is the ideology of the world's working-class people," the inflexible profile intones, and Mother makes one last doomed attempt to build a dam and stem the tide that's steadily been building up: "Why don't I get some dough rising and I can make us some cinnamon rolls."
I swat Mother away the way you would a fly.
"But what's the crux of Marxism, the main idea?"
Father focuses on the TV, but Teija Sopanen is already smiling at the people of Finland and wishing them a good night.

But Father has the silent support of Lenin and Stalin's auburn-colored spines:
"Marxism-Leninism is what it is."
"Excuse me?"
Mother sighs and goes out on the balcony for a secret smoke, away from me and Father and our so-called family peace.
"What you see is what you get. Spirits and gods and ghosts, they've all been invented by the bourgeoisie."

And now

she feels the dazzling glow of victory.

But, afraid her victory will slip through her fingers, she asks, just to be sure:
"So the only thing that exists is what a person can see?"
Father nods, sealing his defeat:
"Whatever I can see myself, that's what exists. Nothing else."

And the winning move made with trembling fingers:
"So what about electricity?"

And Father, preparing for defeat:
"What about it? It's been scientifically proven to exist."

And the death blow:
"But you can't see electricity. And it still exists."
"Nonsense," Father says. "I can see lightbulbs, the TV, my electric razor. They all use electricity."

Her victory drifts off course, but only for a moment.

Now she has two paths.
She starts with the first one:
"Sure, they all use electricity, but you can't see it. It's something you can't see, but it still exists."
"But I can see a lamp. You can see for yourself that it won't work without electricity. Everything uses

BACKLIGHT

electricity. In America they even have electric toothbrushes, in case you didn't know."

And since the first path is too philosophical, I opt for the other, after ignoring the questions from Mother, who's been shivering on the balcony:
"Are you done? Is it safe to come in now?"
"Well what about before electricity was invented? Did it exist then? What does Marx say to that?" I ask.
And

Father smiles the way you do at an idiot:
"Electricity's been around since the Big Bang. People didn't invent electricity, they just invented ways to use it. Edison, he's the one who invented the lightbulb…an Englishman, by the way."
And now

Marxism's death blow:
"So there are forces in the world that people can't see and don't know anything about, like electricity before the lightbulb was invented. I rest my case."
And

the end comes quickly.
Electricity crackles in the air—and Edison has no time to direct it to the ceiling light.
The coffee cup and its dregs fly over the table, followed by spit and a hand balled into a fist. Two exclamations run together:

"Reiskano!"
and
"I'll give this schoolgirl some Marx, perkele!"

Mother gently presses a tea towel rinsed in cold water to my tearful, puffy eyes and to my lip, which to my disappointment isn't nearly swollen enough.

She forcefully swallows the sentence trying to make its way up her throat, which would sound something like: "Didn't I warn you, so many times."

And I swallow the sentence I don't know how to form, which would sound something like:
"But it was worth it."

Still

from that night onward I hate the Caliph, Father, Marx, and God, in that order.

The Captainess gives her a scolding, but she's no longer allowed in the shade of the rubber plant or anywhere near the piano or the cookie trays.

She's reprimanded in her small bedroom where she's been locked up for the past two days to think about her actions, which are beginning to fade from her memory just like the bruise from her neck.

She stands embarrassingly close to the Captainess, swollen from too much sleep and boredom.
An old person's sour odor wafts from the Captainess's mouth, which the Captainess has tried to mask by eating blackcurrant jelly and whipped cream.
The smell makes her dream of home: of the long and endless journey to this room and the impossible journey back.

She listens to the Captainess's scolding, which contains an introduction, a warm-up, and a climax, but she doesn't understand what she hears, even though the Captainess speaks to her in English, because

now she does regret what she's done, truly and deeply, even though she doesn't understand what she's done wrong.
And she loves the Captainess, who holds her fate in her hands and is the only living person she's allowed to see.

She is the Captainess's prisoner—she wants to be.
She has no other choice.
"Do you understand?"

She nods.
She hasn't understood a word of what the Captainess said, but she thinks, rationally, that in the next few days the Captainess's words will surely become flesh.
And they

did:
I was allowed to stay, but I was demoted to the kitchen.
All my evenings off were canceled.
The Captainess reallocated them for a vacation I would get to spend in August with the Captainess's family, including Kurt, Dorre, the Captain, and the Captainess herself, on a road trip to Lake Thun—since the Captainess didn't want to be responsible for letting someone leave the country without having ever seen Lake Thun to spread who knows what kinds of opinions.

I was allowed to stay after assuring the Captainess that

BACKLIGHT

I wouldn't say a word about Switzerland until I'd seen Lake Thun or engage in any further inappropriate activities or raise my voice against God or invoke Switzerland's labor laws.

It was Tante Irma's birthday, and Tante Dolores organized a party.

We sat by the pool, the birthday cake blazing with countless candles against the darkening sky.
We sang "Give Me Faith like Daniel" hand in hand, and Tante Irma, the birthday girl, had to slap a flushed Daniel who was jumping up and down from too much excitement.
"This song has nothing to do with you. This song is about the real Daniel who didn't lose his courage even when he was thrown to the lions, because God was with Daniel, the real Daniel, and never left his side."

After we'd finished singing hand in hand and I'd thought of my distant homeland, where we sing songs in minor keys about death and entire generations fading into oblivion, it was time for the presents.

Tante Irma received a beautiful Hungarian box of chocolates (which I'd seen Miklos's mother bring for her son); a bottle of cloudberry liquor from me, which I'd hidden in my closet for a special occasion; lots of hand-picked flowers and drawings from the children; and a dress.

The dress had short sleeves and was made with an op art print fabric: black geometric shapes intertwined with white geometric shapes in such a way that anyone not used to the optical pattern got a headache and felt queasy.
The dress had a geometrically inspired neckline, and a perfumed fabric rose was fastened to it with a safety pin.

Tante Irma was thrilled to receive such a multipurpose dress: without the rose it was a practical everyday dress, and with it, it became an excellent party dress.

Tante Irma was equally thrilled that Tante Dolores, who had given her the op art surprise, was wearing the exact same dress.

Tante Irma and Tante Dolores started to wear their matching op art dresses every day, without the roses on weekdays and with the roses on weekends. The two Tantes appeared dispirited on laundry day until they came up with the idea of taking the dresses out of the orphanage's common laundry hamper and washing them themselves.
Tante Dolores's sleeve was folded over Tante Irma's shier sleeve and held it in a clothespin's determined grip.

BACKLIGHT

And every two weeks the op art dresses swayed to the same rhythm on the clothesline, in the same breeze that flapped the singing von Trapp family's pants and skirts.

I didn't have a dress made from op art fabric, and I didn't have a single friend in the entire orphanage.

A girl named Anna replaced Renate, but no one spoke to her because she came from Torino.
I didn't talk to her either, since she didn't understand German or English and I didn't understand Italian.

Renate did send me a letter from southern Switzerland, but the Captainess didn't care to give it to me; Tante Dolores told me so at the dinner table, in a whisper.
Tante Dolores had managed to read enough of the letter as it lay open under the rubber plant to tell me Renate had written that there were no islands in southern Switzerland, and that part of the country wasn't even by the ocean, as Renate had thought.

I was allowed to take the children to the nearby woods once a day for some exercise.

The woods were meticulously maintained, and the trails were attractively sprinkled with sand.
Any rocks that could have tripped hikers were neatly piled off to the side.
You weren't allowed to stray off the paths or to pick any flowers, pinecones, or fallen branches.

You weren't allowed to bring anything extra that didn't belong in the woods, and you weren't allowed to take anything out, except your own trash.

The fir-scented forest stood faithfully by the side of the road; it swallowed little Hansels and Gretels into its depths for the prescribed two hours, and then it spit them out again with flushed cheeks, refreshed and calm.

The op art dresses excited Tante Irma and Tante Dolores, who insisted on joining us on our outings.

The Tantes no longer cared to go see if the raspberries or blackberries were ripe; instead they walked far ahead of the children, whispering together hand in hand; they nudged one another off the path, blew on the other's scratches, and gave each other playful pecks on the cheek and neck.

At the dinner table, the Tantes kicked each other and exchanged forks, and Tante Dolores let a hairy piece of meat that was coquettishly perched on Tante Irma's extended fork tickle her upper lip.
Tante Irma burst out laughing, smothered it with her napkin, and accidentally kicked me under the table.
I kicked back, hard, and tried to catch the Captainess's eye.
The Captainess's eyes roved around the dining room as steadily as a lighthouse's beacon, but when Tante Irma dropped her fork and disappeared under the table to get it, the eyes stopped at her empty chair.

BACKLIGHT

Tante Irma pinched me painfully under the table, and as the Captainess's eyes had stopped so close to me, I winced in agony.

The Captainess looked right at me.

I smiled apologetically and glanced at the empty chair, but then the Captainess shook her head, so slightly it could have been mistaken for a Parkinson's tremor.

Later I lingered by the door to the dining room, and when the Captainess passed me, I shook my head, so imperceptibly that only the Captainess could see it.
The Captainess smiled with one corner of her mouth, so imperceptibly that only I could see it.
But

it's not until evening that the Captainess asks for me, and she's not under the rubber plant—I've lost that and the piano playing and the lace curtains fluttering in the breeze forever.

The Captainess speaks to me in the linen closet, where we're surrounded by clean nightgowns, stacks of sweet-smelling diapers, and sheets stamped with the Salvation Army's logo in German.

Her speech includes an introduction, a warm-up, a climax, and a conclusion.

And this time I listen to the Captainess so carefully that I understand everything she says and almost everything she leaves unsaid:

"When you came into our home from a country unknown to us, we believed we were employing a good and proper girl. I can tell you now that you came warmly recommended by high-ranking majors in the Finnish Salvation Army. We are open-minded people, we're certainly trying to be, and we believed those recommendations, which seemed so sincere.
"There have been unexpected difficulties along the way, I admit that, as I'm sure you do too, and we've diligently said our prayers in order to preserve our faith in you and the Finnish Salvation Army.
"And I believe our prayers have been answered. It seems to me that you are a very good girl at heart. When a girl your age goes out in the world on her own, the temptations—the influence of bad company and the overestimation of her own character, among others—are surely great.
"I respect your mother, who has had the courage to send her teenage daughter into the world to test her mettle. My Dorre is four years older than you, and I still wouldn't have the courage to put her in an unpredictable situation, though of course we have no need to, since Dorre lives in a country with plenty of opportunities for hard-working young people."
And

BACKLIGHT

as a result of the Captainess's conclusion, Tante Irma and I pack our things and exchange rooms that evening: Tante Irma gets my room upstairs, and I move into the room next to Tante Dolores downstairs.

That night my dreams torment me like mosquitos, and I keep waking up to their bite.

The house is quiet.
The moon hangs over the woods, and I'm hungry.
I've done as the Captainess has urged me to and eaten my fill at dinner, even though the meal consisted of fried liver and steamed brussels sprouts.

But I'm still hungry.
I want to taste thick multigrain bread and jam full of sugar and whole blackberries on my tongue again.
I try to resist temptation, as the Captainess has urged me to, but as that has never been my strong suit, I give in.
I sneak into the kitchen, cut two slices of crusty bread, and spread fat on them—it's too soft to be butter, but it tastes too much like butter to be margarine.
I put some jam in an empty jar I find in the children's section of the pantry.
I hide my haul under my robe and sneak back to my new room.

A faint light shines under Tante Dolores's door.

It's shockingly red.

I hear whispers, laughter, a cough.
Then it's ominously quiet.

I try to sneak silently past the door, but it's flung open.

Tante Dolores stands before me, brilliantly backlit.

"*Guten Abend*," I say, as I try to keep my arm holding the buttered bread pressed to my side.
Tante Dolores slams the door shut and says something to someone in a low voice.
The only word I can make out is *Idiot*, and I'm afraid it refers to me.

I'm afraid Tante Dolores has noticed my unnatural posture and knows that I have buttered bread and blackberry jam under my gown, and that she'll tell the other person in the room who will in turn tell the Captainess.

I don't dare eat my snack; I'm not hungry anymore anyway.
I pick up my dictionary and start formulating an apology in the light of the moon, just in case.

I think I should be able to appeal to the Captainess's impressions of my faraway homeland: the destitute circumstances and the nutrient-deficient food, which

can make a person look chubby even though they are chronically undernourished and always hungry.
I've found the word for *nutrition* in my dictionary and am just about to look for *poor* when I hear someone shriek in Tante Dolores's room.

My first thought:
Tante Dolores is torturing a child whom she's tied to her bed or the radiator.
The second:
Tante Dolores has slit her wrist with a razor and shrieked at the sight of blood.
And my third, lifesaving thought:
There must be a man in Tante Dolores's room.

If Tante Dolores has a man in her room, then she'll keep her lips sealed.

Tante Dolores will keep her lips sealed if she has a man in her room and knows that I know there's a man in her room.

I press my ear to the wall.
It's quiet in Tante Dolores's room.
I open my wardrobe door, pull out my clothes, and throw them on the bed.
I take out the shelves.

And I'm right: the wardrobe's been positioned against the door connecting Tante Dolores's and my rooms.

I climb inside.

I sit in the wardrobe.
The moon shines into my bedroom and onto the bread and jam I've left on my desk.
It's quiet in Tante Dolores's room, and I get hungry again.

I'm on way out to get my snack when I hear a shriek behind the blocked door.

But it isn't Tante Dolores—it's Tante Irma.

Tante Dolores shushes her; there's faint tittering and then Tante Irma's whisper:
"*Aber es tut weh.*"

Weh. What did that mean again? *Weh tun*, to make something hurt.

But it hurts.

And it's only now

that the truth is revealed to her as a hot and breathless shame that torments her.

Tante Irma is Tante Dolores's man.

Or woman.

BACKLIGHT

The beloved lying naked under the sheets with Tante Dolores, who is doing things that hurt Tante Irma and make her shriek and giggle.

She rushes out of the wardrobe and cries out when she bangs her knee on a corner.
A hiss comes from the other side of the wall.
Then it's quiet.

The moon shines into the room and onto her as she sits in the middle of the floor crying with rage, though she doesn't know why.

the dance of death

Daylight shines on the felt roofing. My knees and palms are burning.

I'm hiding.
But I hope I'll be found quickly.

Aunt Kaarina carries a tray with juice and slices of cardamom bread sweating in the heat to the two lawn chairs.
From the roof all I can see are two straw hats and four long, brown legs.

The sun paints fleeting heart-shaped lights on the surface of the lake.
The leaves on the birch trees refuse to stir, just like the four legs lying on the lawn chairs.
Aunt Kaarina says something—I can't hear what—and looks around her.

Aunt Kaarina is looking for me.
I scooch behind the chimney and lie down.

Now the felt roofing burns my thighs too, and my elbows. Someone says something to Aunt Kaarina—again I can't hear what—and Aunt Kaarina leaves the tray on the table and goes inside; she, too, stops looking for me.

I've ended up on the roof of the Pollari's summer cottage as the result of the following chain of events:

Mother was worried when I still showed no sign of a tan by mid-July.
She decided to call Aunt Kaarina and ask if Uncle Tauno's sciatica, which Mother embarrassingly mispronounces, had gotten any better.
The sunny summer weather was praised on both ends of the line, and there was sighing about teenagers who didn't have the energy to swim or bike or take walks and who spent all their time sulking inside with their noses buried in books even though...
And the *even though* was followed by a long litany of all the things carried in front of young ladies' noses, starting with Helena's Camping-brand bicycle and ending with expensive tuition fees and a swimsuit bought for me from Stockmann's department store, which only used half a yard's worth of material but cost as much as one of Mother's fully lined dresses.
And before Mother got Aunt Kaarina to invite me to their summer cottage for two weeks to swim in my expensive swimsuit and go bicycling and jogging with

BACKLIGHT

Helena, they reminisced about those years before the wars when girls who were Helena's and my age, as Mother and Aunt Kaarina were then, spent their summers working as maids.
"Or in factories," Mother reminded Aunt Kaarina. "Like me for example."
Another example came from the other end of the line, and

two days later I found myself sitting on a bus with my swimsuit, a change of clothes, and a packet of Paulig coffee in my bag.
I got off at the agreed-upon stop, but Helena wasn't there waiting for me as promised.
I sat down on the milk churn stand. A poster of the round-faced Markus Allan was pinned to it with thumbtacks.

I waited an hour and then half an hour more.

I seethed with rage, hating Markus Allan and Finnish tango, but I couldn't drift away from that time and place into an Arabian night or the role of Charlotta Ivanovna in Anton P. Chekhov's *The Cherry Orchard* at the Finnish National Theater.

I was too eager to see Helena in all her blonde beauty.

And when Helena finally arrived, sweating on her bike, I saw Allu riding behind her.
Allu was Helena's best friend.

I didn't have a bicycle or a best friend, and to top it all off, Helena, who was just as blonde and dimpled as ever, had changed her name to Lila.
Allu whispered that Aunt Kaarina and Uncle Tauno, and even the principal at Helena's school, all called Helena Lila these days, and the county board was drawing up the papers, which, in due course, would certify that no Helena had ever existed.

Helena had become someone else, but I hadn't, and as I stumbled at a half-run behind the two rear wheels flinging gravel at me, I cursed Mother and Aunt Kaarina and the sweltering work-filled summers of the '30s, which I'd now have to pay for in my own Siberia.

I find a shady spot behind the chimney that doesn't burn my thighs.
I stay there, for now.

Smoke swirls from the chimney.
The oven door clatters inside the house.
Then the front door opens, and Aunt Kaarina goes to the sauna to get two aluminum pails; from behind me on my left, I hear the even creaking sound of the water pump.

The straw hats don't move, but two hands stretch out from the lawn chairs at the same time to take their own glasses of juice.

"Are you deaf?"
That's Lila, not Helena, who then says:
"Hey, for real!"

The pump stops.
Aunt Kaarina:
"What is it?"
"The cable!"

The pump starts creaking again.
Then I see Aunt Kaarina half-run to the sauna with a full bucket in each hand and come out a moment later. Aunt Kaarina pulls an electric cable from the sauna to the lawn chairs, plugs it into the transistor radio next to the juice pitcher, and again,
for maybe the thousandth time this week, I hear The Beatles from the crackling speakers: "I'll send all my lovin' to you…"

I press my hands to my ears and wish the straw hats could see my gesture, but they don't budge.
And then

I see the spider.

It's an orb weaver.

I've never seen an orb weaver before, not even a picture,

but I know that's what this is.
It has monstrously long legs and a mark on its back that foreshadows death.

It doesn't foreshadow death.
It *is* death.

It moves in the air between the chimney and the felt roofing.
It dances its own strange and horrifying choreography in the empty air, and then the web is finished.
It moves to the side, close to my elbow, which feels cold and paralyzed despite the heat.
The spider shows me the cross on its back.

A brimstone butterfly lands on the back of my hand.
I can see its antennae testing the air, and it startles me.
I shake my hand, and the butterfly, in its yellow totality, falls into the spider's web.
The butterfly struggles in the web, but the spider wastes no time.
It clumsily but quickly crosses its web and strikes below the yellow wings flailing like distress flags, and

I don't see the end because I hide my face in my hands, in the smell of sweat, roofing, and horror.

The macaroni casserole is ready, The Beatles have gone silent, and three voices call for me.

BACKLIGHT

I come down from the roof.
The flagstones leading from the porch to the sauna are burning hot.
But the grass is cool underfoot, and I'm not in any danger anyway;

I've also become someone else.
I've just experienced the first metaphor of my life.

I'm the one who sees, even if I don't want to; I'm the one who hears, even if I press my hands to my ears.
I'm the one who causes death and is horrified by it.

I need to tell the Captainess about Tante Irma and Tante Dolores and their secret…

But I can't find the words for it, not even in Finnish.
Is it love?
A relationship?
A love affair?
Or a sinful relationship? No, that sounds too biblical.
A sexual relationship?
That sounds like it's from a gynecology textbook.

I need to tell the Captainess about the relationship between Tante Irma and Tante Dolores, which they themselves seem to think is a love affair (titter), for the following reasons:

Their relationship is unhealthy, *nicht gesund*.
In fact it's sick, *krank, sehr krank*.

No.
The conclusion is one the Captainess will have to come

to herself.
I need to tell the Captainess about the relationship between Tante Irma and Tante Dolores (titter), which they themselves seem to think is a love affair (no, put the titter here) for the following reasons:

We care for underage children, and...
No, that's too obvious.
We are responsible for children, so...
Would the Captainess be insulted?
After all, the Captainess is well aware that she is the one who's primarily responsible for the children, and after her the responsibility passes to the rest of us, like me and Tante Dolores and Tante Irma...

The moon shines into my room and onto my dictionary and the wardrobe, muddling my mind.
I'm in a labyrinth, and I can't find my way out.

I'm Theseus without Ariadne's red thread, and a monstrous Minotaur with four labia is wallowing in its own fluids behind the wardrobe.

Or is it?
Did I understand those three words, those three incredibly short German words, correctly?

Is what I think Tante Irma and Tante Dolores are doing generally possible?
And is it common?

BACKLIGHT

Do people in Switzerland do this every night?
Does the phrase *gut geschlafen* allude exactly to this?

If this is a completely normal activity, I'd make a fool of myself with my revelation.
No, it would be even worse.
I'd strip myself naked in front of the Captainess, because even if the Captainess didn't ask me out loud, she would certainly ask herself: *Why does this girl find this so interesting?*

The moon shines, and she makes a decision that's flattering to herself.
She decides to give Tante Dolores and Tante Irma the opportunity to prove their innocence.
And she decides to give the Captainess the chance to prove her ignorance.

Dark, heavy clouds hang over the Alps, the chapel, and the orphanage in the morning.
I think it's a sign, even though Tante Dolores and Tante Irma drink their café crème in their op art dresses as if nothing at all has happened.
The Captainess doesn't appear at the breakfast table.
Kurt announces that the Captainess has a migraine, eliciting a sympathetic stir in the room, and that the Captain himself is tending to his wife with cold compresses and warm prayers.

Tante Dolores glances at Tante Irma.
Now I'm convinced.

I won't allow myself to be fooled anymore.
And although Tante Irma doesn't even glance at Tante Dolores, I hear rustling under the table.
Tante Irma kicks Tante Dolores. Tante Dolores has gotten her answer: the day is theirs.
And

an hour later there's an announcement in the nursery: Tante Dolores has also gotten a migraine—it must be the low-pressure system—and Tante Irma has retreated to Tante Dolores's room to tend to her with cold compresses and warm prayers.

In the evening I retreat into my wardrobe with my snack in good time, and in less than two hours, my patience is rewarded.
Tante Dolores's door opens, and I hear Tante Irma's voice, then an hour of quiet whispering, rustling paper, and vague sounds; the thumping sound of chair legs—or is it the bed?—and then the incriminating:
"*Liebling*."

I step out of the wardrobe, not caring if the Tantes hear me or not.

The moon isn't shining.
It's raining, and I begin to feel the first inklings of a

migraine in my own temples.
But I don't care about that; with the help of my dictionary, I focus on drafting an account of the events that have led me to prepare this report.

My report has an introduction, a warm-up, a climax, and a conclusion.

The introduction:
I come from a country that may undoubtedly seem primitive, and even strange, to those who have enjoyed a safe and independent existence in the heart of Europe for many hundreds of years. People in these countries, take Switzerland for example, have never experienced war, shortages, freezing winters, or mass migration to Sweden.

The warm-up:
However, there are things we take for granted in countries like Finland.
People have the right to go out in nature and pick berries and mushrooms and fish and hunt, which I personally don't care for.
You can also engage in these activities on someone else's land, unlike in other countries like Switzerland where parks are called forests, and real forests are gated with signs that say *Verboten. Privat.*
In the despised country I come from, we actually do live in finished houses, just like people do in other places, Switzerland for example, and no one rides around on

reindeer these days, except for Joulupukki—that's Santa Claus—who lives in Finland in a place called Korvatunturi, and not in Sweden as the Swedes like to claim.
Finland may not have cantons, but Finland was the first country in Europe to give women the right to vote. And Finnish women vote in every single election, just like I will when I turn twenty-one.
And there are other important things about Finland, which I will now share in my climax.

And the climax:
Not everyone in Finland wants to get married, including myself and other people in my generation. It may seem odd to those of you who are forced to live abroad (chuckle here to lighten the mood).
It's just as odd to us, and to me for example, that women have love affairs with each other (laugh if you can), and to top it all off, that they have children in their care who may not always be true orphans but who can't sleep well because they're cared for by women who claim that a jar of jam is hot when it is in fact cold and who kiss each other because there are no men around.

And the conclusion:
If you, my dear Captainess, have known all along that this is going on in your orphanage, and if you, my dear Captainess, have decided not to intervene despite your knowledge of this affair, I must leave and go work at the chocolate factory in Bern—even though I've been recommended to you by high-ranking

majors in Finland—and report this to the newspapers.

There's a shy knock on my door.
I ignore it.
Only after the third knock do I open the door a crack.

Tante Dolores stands in the hallway, brilliantly backlit, and she hands me a box of chocolates.

"You aren't sleeping either. It's this terrible low-pressure system."

It's a Hungarian box of chocolates.
I put it in my suitcase, and

it will be my gift to Lentsu, who will pick me up at Helsinki's South Harbor when this is all over.

We're standing in the linen closet again, the Captainess and I.
The Captainess is in a hurry, a mask on her face and a nursing bottle tucked under her arm; she's warming it for René who has chicken pox; she won't let anyone else care for him, especially not a foreigner, since the disease can adversely affect the testicles.

I can only see the Captainess's eyes, and I find it hard to start my speech, the outline of which is burning in one of the teeny tiny pockets of my Marimekko dress.

It seems inappropriate to start with Finland and reindeer, and I'm so flustered I can't remember what Joulupukki—I mean Santa Claus—has to do with Tante Dolores's and Tante Irma's sexual relationship.

"Tante Dolores," I say, starting from the wrong part of my speech, and I see a metallic gleam in the Captainess's eyes.

I don't know how to go on.

"Tante Irma," I try again, and the Captainess takes the nursing bottle from under her arm, shakes a drop onto the back of her hand, and finishes my aborted sentence for me:
"…are both extremely good caregivers."
"Yes," I hasten to add. "And. And, and, but," and I laugh in the entirely wrong place.
"The children like them," I hear from behind the mask, and I say:
"Yes, yes, but…"
The Captainess is entirely focused on assessing the temperature of the liquid in the nursing bottle.
I grope in my Marimekko pockets, but it's no use because the Captainess is on her way out; she opens the door and is already in the hallway when she turns to me and takes off her mask:
"The Captain has decided that you can manage house

BACKLIGHT

number three on your own while Tante Sigfrid is on vacation."

On the same day the Captain trims the poplar in the yard into the shape of an upside-down ice cream cone, and Miklos's mother is deported from Switzerland, and Tantes Irma, Dolores, Sigfrid, and Pirkko lose their source of Hungarian chocolates;
the same day an arsonist sets Münsingen's church on fire, and eighteen protestors are arrested in Paris;
the same day Brigitte, another new girl, who doesn't know German and swears in French, cries inconsolably and is carried out to the front hall, and Anna from Torino falls ill with a rare form of diphtheria;
the same day I carry my suitcase decorated with the Mosfilm logo into house number three—a Salvation Army van stops in front of the swimming pool.

Tante Irma throws her bag along with the lunch the Captainess herself has prepared for her in the back of the van; she jumps in the passenger seat and glances up at Tante Dolores's window where the curtains flutter; but she doesn't take her handkerchief out until the van has turned onto Standwegen road toward town, so that I barely catch a glimpse of it.

I lie in Tante Sigfrid's bed, on the clean sheets of house number three.

The clock strikes in the living room, two fateful times. Brigitte cries in French in her dreams, and the moon shines shamelessly through the blinds.

single people

My godfather was the first to get one, followed by Arska Lehtonen half a year later.
Then it was Leka Westerholm and Eko Kalervo's turn. Eko Turunen got his at the end of August, and then two months later, in October, it was Father's turn; all the men in Father's cycling club were turning forty-five that year.

Father's soda siphon was dark purple and so clear you could see your reflection in it.
The ice bucket was cut crystal. It reminded me of Grandma's sugar bowl, except that the ice bucket had a silver handle with Father's initials engraved on it.

Father diligently walked back and forth between the kitchen and the living room with the ice bucket in hand, looking like a berry picker.

On Saturday evenings, the siphons sprayed water into whiskey glasses, which were also new in the households.

Tongs delicately picked out ice cubes and dropped them into the whiskey.
There was the sound of clinking glasses, light sighs, and the striking of a match as cigarillos were lit, and then:
"Now one more thing about Austin cars…"

The women drank liqueur in the living room, either Marlin's Cloudberry or Arctic Raspberry, and giggled behind their paper napkins as they traded photographs.
"Oh God, I don't remember that at all."
Cardamom buns were no longer served at these get-togethers.
"There's no point forcing them on people. Modern folks just don't care for cardamom buns anymore," Mother said, arranging Ipnos crackers topped with butter and slices of Kreivi Bergkäse cheese, onion sausage, and pickles on a serving platter.
"Modern women prefer salty over sweet," Mother announced. "Men and children, now, they don't care for candy or salty things anymore."

And the modern women quickly hide the photographs in their purses when the doorbell rings.
"Who could that be, at this hour?" Mother asks with concern, and from the kitchen doorway, Father, who has escaped from the world of Opels, Citroëns, and Peugeots to get some fresh air, says:
"Who the Devil would show up at this hour?"

It's Aunt Ulla.

BACKLIGHT

She walks with difficulty, her legs spread wide.
"I've got to go to the bathroom, fast. Lord have mercy. Pirkko, get over here and help me."

The modern women go pale, and Aunt Ulla and I shut ourselves in the bathroom.
And

all's quiet on the other side of the door as I pull up Aunt Ulla's skirt.
She's tied an extra pair of pantyhose around her waist, and she pulls a bottle of Ballantine's Whiskey out of each leg.
"Can you imagine what it was like trying to walk naturally with these? And then sitting down, first in a tram and then a bus?"

Father pours Ballantine's whiskey for the men and offers Aunt Ulla a goblet of cloudberry liqueur.
And Aunt Ulla:
"Don't give me that sweet stuff. Pour me a double shot. And pour one for Pirkko, too."

And I get my first ever shot of whiskey, from Father's own hand.
It tastes bad, but I swallow it all at once, just like Aunt Ulla does.
And just like Aunt Ulla, I immediately motion to Father

to pour me another with a slight wave of my hand.
"That *häntä* even followed me on the tram. You'd think he'd have better things to do," Aunt Ulla said, lighting a cigarette, just as I would have liked to.
"What *häntä*?" Aunt Tuija asks, and I chuckle just like Aunt Ulla does.
And the whole time Aunt Ulla explains to the modern women that all of Helsinki, including the suburbs, is considered a customs area, and that a *häntä* is an overly eager customs officer who, as the name implies, tails any staff leaving the ship whom they suspect of smuggling, Mother pointedly stares at me in warning.

Mother doesn't want me to start copying everything Aunt Ulla says and does.
That would pretty much guarantee me staying single forever, which Mother thinks I'm heading for as it is.
Being single means no children and a lousy lot in life:
"Just think: what if you have to pay your phone bills and newspaper subscription fees and rent and everything else all on your own?"
And if you don't have any children, you'll ultimately regret it when you're on your deathbed and your life feels meaningless:
"Just when you've managed to scrimp and save something for yourself, strangers'll show up and take it all from you."
"Or acquaintances," I say, and Mother:
"Oh, you think it's funny now, but you just wait and see."

BACKLIGHT

"But how can I see anything if the coffin lid's already been nailed shut when my stuff's being given away?" I'm about to ask, but then I don't.

The men like Aunt Ulla.
The first bottle of Ballantine's is quickly drained, and they forget all about brake fluid.
"When you accelerate, the friction increases, too," my godfather says, and my godmother, innocently:
"Unto sure loves talking about cars."
The men burst out laughing.
Aunt Ulla is on her fourth glass of whiskey and takes no notice of the siphon owners who are no longer content to stay in the kitchen and are instead swarming at the door, pushing and shoving each other.
But Mother notices, and I notice that Mother notices: I can tell by her clenched jaw and her determined effort to change the subject without offending anyone.

And Mother notices that I've noticed that she's noticed that Aunt Ulla's cast a spell over the entire evening, an evening with other couples that was supposed to be fun and carefree, where no one would feel slighted or left out.
Mother notices I've noticed because of my gleeful expression.

She realizes I'm tempting the fate she herself has imagined for me.

What's an annual newspaper subscription fee next to the look of horror and adoration on my godmother's face as she glances shyly at my whiskey-gulping aunt twirling a Marlboro between her long red nails?
And what's a widow's pension next to seeing grown men regress into competitive little boys?

And when the men, flushed from the whiskey, fight to help Aunt Ulla into her Karakul fur coat in the entryway full of blue cigar smoke, there's a hint of revenge in the air, right when the women thrust the stack of photographs into Mother's hand.
"These are yours. Nepe made copies for everyone. Don't go showing them around."

"Well, we got that out of the way," Father says as he sits down in his armchair and takes off his wristwatch.

That's what Father always says after company leaves.

And now that it's just the three of us, he takes one last little shot and gets more ice from the freezer to put in his ice bucket; he squirts water from his siphon into his glass and lights a North State cigarette.
Mother opens the door to the balcony and the vent window in the bedroom to air out the apartment before we go to bed, and then she slips the photographs into the top drawer of Father's desk where

I know to look for them as soon as I come home from

school on Monday, and I bring them to the ship where Aunt Ulla works in the galley.

"Yep, I'm sailing with the dishwater," Aunt Ulla says.

The photographs are from Eko Turunen's birthday party.
They mostly show various limbs and furniture, and hands with splayed fingers held up to the camera.
The mouths are saying: *Don't* or *Now* or *Not now* or *Picture*.
In one of them Father is on all fours in his polyester pants on the Turunen's imitation pile rug; his glasses are askew, and Aunt Nepe is riding on his back and swinging his tie.

Aunt Ulla quickly flips through the pictures and throws them on the galley table.

"How shameful. My word, when you think about it. The kind of life they're leading."
We drink our coffee, a couple of free women, and I try to keep from coughing as I take drags on Aunt Ulla's Marlboro.
"Couples form their own dictatorship in this world," Aunt Ulla says. "If you pay attention, you'll see that couples only invite other couples over. Everyone has fun as long as there isn't a single person around. Single people don't have partners to rely on, even our Unto goes on about it, blah blah this and blah blah that. And then Unto says he can't come because his wife Sisko doesn't approve if he does this or that. Single people

have to answer for their words and actions themselves. When a single person shows up, everyone else becomes single in a way. A single person is a threat to their environment."

I'd like to be threat to my environment.

I announce to my environment that I'm single.

"There's no point in worrying about that just yet, dear child," Mother says, before sharing the following piece of wisdom passed down through the generations:
"You never know what branch the Devil's gonna be sitting on. That's what my late mother always said."
And Father:
"I've always wondered why people talk about dead people saying this or that. People do and say things when they're alive, not when they're dead. The dead don't say anything."
And Grandpa:
"Well then. I think I'll go lie down."

I need to be a bigger threat to my environment.
So, I announce that I absolutely, without any doubt, plan to remain single for the rest of my life.

And Mother:
"You're not doing that to me, not giving me any grandkids. Seeing as I only got one kid myself."
"Yeah, and look how she turned out," Father announces.

And I say:
"What do you mean? Could you be more specific?"
And Mother:
"Don't start again, or I'm leaving."
"Where do you think you're going?" Father asks, winking at me. "Remember how Tuija Lehtonen left?"
And

ensconced in his armchair behind his soda siphon, Father launches into his impressive story about the time Tuija Lehtonen got angry with Arska, her one-armed husband, and packed her things, planning to move in with her mother in Turku. But Tuija started to regret her decision as soon as she got on the tram to go to the train station. After all, how could someone with only one arm manage without a wife? And so Tuija jumped off the tram and went right back home ready to forgive Arska, but before going inside, she decided to peek in the window first to see just how depressed Arska looked. But as it turned out, Arska was whistling away, frying eggs on their gas stove, and Tuija got angry all over again and jumped back on the tram. This time she made it all the way to the train station. But the last train to Turku had already left, and since Tuija had no place to stay, she had to go on back home and stay there.

The fact that I'm single clearly isn't eliciting any interest or even bewilderment.

People have seen me as single for a long time, maybe even since I was born.

It seems obvious to everyone that I am, and will remain, single.
It seems obvious to everyone except me, and suddenly it begins to terrify me.

I no longer see much of Ritva, who is dating someone whose name I can't remember.
But I do remember, bitterly, that his native language is Swedish and that he plays jazz on the piano with a cigarette hanging from his lips, looking like the late James Dean—I mean he looks like James Dean before he became the late James Dean.

Eikku, who goes to dances with me at the Helsinki Hall of Culture on Saturdays, doesn't have a boyfriend, but she has her pick every time we go.
I have no doubt that Eikku will pair up as soon as she finds the right candidate whose zodiac sign aligns with her demanding Sagittarius personality: she wants to devote herself to someone but remain completely independent at the same time.

I stand next to Eikku in the row of girls waiting to be asked to dance, and I try to soften my look of abject terror by laughing at the boys who've styled their hair with Brylcreem.
When tangos like "Satumaa" or "Geranium Tango"

burst into their metallic, dragging tempo, and the row of girls moves a few feet closer to the row of boys, I move too. And I try not to look at anyone, just like the girls who get asked to dance do.

No one asks me to dance.

In the bathroom I compare myself to the girls who get picked and the girls who don't.
I have more in common with the girls who are picked than with those who aren't, because the girls who are never picked are either drunk or horribly fat—or else their faces are covered in pimples.
I have a fuller but still normal figure, I'm wearing the clothes Mother has chosen for me, and I have curls from twisting my hair in curlers overnight.

I can't understand how 500 boys with Brylcreem-styled hair can all simultaneously recognize that I'm single, one Saturday night after another.

So I've humiliated myself by announcing that I'm single to my environment.
It's landed not as a threat but a confession: a plea for pity and understanding.

I've lowered my weapons before I've even had the chance to pick them up.
And now

I have two choices before me: I can try to pair up with someone, or I can make people jealous of my approach to being single.

Aunt Ulla's approach to being single doesn't feel like enough.
She throws it to me lightly, in passing, when we're leaning on the chain-link fence at Käpylä racetrack and hoping the horse we've bet on with the last of Aunt Ulla's money will win:
"Personally I've always appreciated the company of women more than men. You can laugh at anything with women, and you can do things like play the lottery or bet on horses together. You can spend a great evening with a woman without her demanding that you iron her shirt the next morning. Women are just more decent all around, no matter what people say."

Mother's approach to being in a couple doesn't seem all that great either:
"Well, Reiska is what he is, but I can't say I regret getting married. At least he doesn't drink or batter his family like so many men do. And he doesn't squander all our money going out at night. And it's nice to have someone to talk to, you know about what your day's been like and so on."

Luckily there are single women like Joan of Arc and Mata Hari and Queen Christina of Sweden, played by Greta Garbo in the movie.

And above all, there's Margarita Volodina who played the commissar in the leather jacket in the movie *Optimistic Tragedy*.

Of course I'd rather be burned at the stake than die in Maria Hospital hooked up to all kinds of tubes like Grandma did.
I'd love to be a spy, if only I knew who to spy for and who to spy on.
And of course I'd wear a leather jacket and sacrifice my life to communism, if God would only agree to release me from the grip of His talons.

I can't become a commissar, or even the president of Finland's Communist Party, because I believe in God.
And I can't become a nun, or even a missionary, because I don't believe in God.

I have to wait for my story to finish writing itself.
I have to believe my life will become a story that will solve my being single.

I have to believe my life will become a story.
And

I do.

No I don't.

redemption

She's read Dostoevsky's *The Idiot* and Nikos Kazantzakis's *Saint Francis*.
And after reading *Saint Francis*, she wrote her first poem, about Saint Francis of Assisi, and herself:

A cave with walls sweating in suffering, salt walls.
A man.
Eyes burning with hunger and a mouth hot from fasting,
a mouth hot from fasting.
And out of the blue glow rises a man, the world's largest penis,
uncontrollable.
Until a flower opens,
soluble in the sun.

She reads her writers carefully—she reads them in fear for her life.

She's gleaned that God is no lamb you can shear for fun; rather God is a lion whose mouth reeks of blood. Following Kazantzakis, she's challenged God to a duel: *Show me the mountain, and I will climb up to the summit.*

God laughs with His bloody mouth and answers ambiguously as He always does: *Climb the mountain, and I will show you the way.*

There are thousands of mountains, almost all of them pointless, and all of them unpredictable.
And she has to climb them all to find the single mountain that's the right one.
God knows that, and that's why God laughs and reeks of blood.

Father has cleared a spot for the soda siphon, ice bucket, and bottle of Leijona whiskey on the bookshelf under Lenin's *Collected Works*.
There they wait from Sunday morning to the next Saturday evening, that is, until Father starts reaching for the siphon on weekday evenings, too.

"He's under a lot of pressure right now," Mother explains when we're alone in the kitchen.
She stores the cucumber slices, the block of Edam cheese, and the leftover meatballs in her brand-new Tupperware containers, one for each type of food, and she tightly presses the well-designed lids on.
I'm also under a lot of pressure, but I can't talk about

that in the kitchen or anywhere else.

We have a new boy in our class called Mara. He's a believer, but his hair is pretty long, he has unshaved peach fuzz on his cheeks, and he wears a shabby parka.
Mara doesn't look like a believer, and he doesn't want to because:
"God doesn't care what people look like. He cares about what's inside."

Mara found God in Hakaniemi—the same building where the Finland–Soviet Union Society is located—in an office on the seventh floor.

"You should come by sometime," Mara says. "Jesus is there every Saturday evening. Believe me."

"The Finland–Soviet Union Society is undergoing a tough restructuring process now that President Kekkonen has stopped handing out government aid," Mother whispers to me from behind her coffee cup.
But the living room is listening:
"Kekkonen is hard on the bourgeoisie too, when he's in the mood. I've seen it so many times."
"Stop going on about that already," Mother yells back. "And keep your hands off that siphon so you can go pick up Airi."
But Father has already squirted water from the siphon into his glass.

"Kekkonen is working on behalf of Finnish industry, and that's good in principle. He's a smart fox anyhow, that Kekkonen, he's pushing big business. The garment industry's a real draw. The Soviets may have rubles, but they don't have the goods."
"It's clear who the secretary-general will be," Mother explains. "The top spot's reserved for someone educated in Moscow, so Topi Karvonen will continue in the role. Now there's a real communist for you. He ate two pounds worth of those Ukrainian apples, the ones that were so bitter and bruised that not even a wolf would touch them. But Topi now, he ate them and went so far as to claim that they were good, sweet even."

It's a Saturday evening in December.
Airi, who Mother looked after in Varkaus before the war years—even though Mother was in need of being looked after herself in those days—called earlier to tell us she's coming to Helsinki for an appointment with a specialist.

Father, the Moskvitch, and I are due to pick up Airi from the train station along with Hanna Partanen's *kalakukko*, a specialty from the Savo region that is surely in Airi's bag and on its way to Finland's capital when God intervenes in His own special and unpredictable way.

The phone rings.
It's a short call. All Father says, three times, is:

BACKLIGHT

"I see. All right then."

Father's fallen to second position, or if you count the general-secretary position, to third.

"Treasurer," Father says, spraying his siphon until his whiskey froths with yellow foam. "Perkele. That sounds like I'm going to be washing the boys' shirts and ironing them, too."
"Well, those accounting courses of yours will come in handy now," Mother says soothingly as she hides the whiskey bottle behind Lenin's works. "And that's what people know you for, for your skills as a businessman. Nothing would come of our store without you."
"I'm changing the title to director of finance," Father says, throwing the Lenins on the floor. He slams the bottle of whiskey on the table and lights a North State cigarette.
"I'm gonna submit the paperwork as soon as I get in to work on Monday."
And Mother:
"Pirkko, come into the kitchen, would you."

And in the kitchen:
"We can't let this director here get behind the wheel. You go on and meet Airi at the station."

There's still almost four hours before Airi is due to arrive and only three-quarters of an hour before Jesus is due to appear in Hakaniemi.

I leave immediately.

The office smells of weak tea and stencil paper.

The shelves are lined with binders, and young people with bad skin and glasses and anoraks fit for the backcountry swarm among them, speaking softly.
I don't see Mara.

I'm just about to turn and leave when someone thrusts a cup of tea in one of my hands and a plate with a rusk in the other.
"Sugar?"
I shake my head, and:
"You must be the seeker Mara told us about."

I'm led to the first row of benches.
I try to balance my teacup and plate. I don't feel good.

These people have nothing to do with Dostoevsky's and Karantzakis's and my God.

No one's eyes burn with the suffering of a seeker or with the joy of discovery.
They talk about mercy and rusks in the same breath and swallow both like ordinary crumbs.

Karantzakis's, Dostoevsky's, Job's, and my God lurks

somewhere out of reach; He holds mercy like a beetle in his clenched fist and is deaf to all passionate prayer until the person praying breaks down, gives up, and loses hope. And that's when God finally opens His fist and throws His mercy like a bucketful of water on the neck of the astonished person kneeling before Him.

And they gasp for breath in this bath they don't deserve; they shed their previous life like dirty clothes and become someone else.

I want to become someone else.

I have to because the self I do have, which I haven't chosen and which has been a misunderstanding from the very beginning, is shriveling my life into a rusk just like the ones on offer among these binder-lined shelves.

I sit in the first row as if I've become stuck in warm mud. I can't get away, except by closing my eyes and writing a long sentence in my mind: *She had come to the wrong place—she realized it as soon as she arrived—but she couldn't get away because the long journey had exhausted her, and the hymn, though sung off-key, lulled her to sleep, deeper and deeper, to the bottom where aquatic plants danced aimlessly in the cool currents until...*

"Would you, Pirkko, like to receive Jesus Christ as your Savior?"

I'm startled.
I open my eyes.

In front of me is the man summoning me, dressed in casual James jeans and a plaid shirt.

I answer yes, and I harbor a faint, fleeting hope that there'll be time for some philosophical discussion, but my tea cup and plate are snatched from my hands and I feel so many unfamiliar fingers touching my arms, my back, my shoulders, and my head before

she finds herself down on her knees on the waxed floor. Hot hands burn her head, and a prayer rises and falls in steep-crested waves, threatening to drown her.
She tries to stand up, but her legs won't support her.

They're praying for her.
They're calling her name, as promised, and she wants to surrender to the waves.

"Jesus Christ is here, at this moment," a clear voice intones over the thundering waves, and a hand pushes her forehead into the coarse fabric of an office chair.

She's dripping in sweat.
The wave of prayer grows wilder as it thunders around her.
"Jesus Christ!" someone cries shrilly.
"Look, look... Christ is here!"

She obediently opens her eyes and sees the fly of the James jeans in front of her, and through the window, on the other side of the square, an advertisement lit up

BACKLIGHT

in neon: *Moskvitch—Volga*.
She quickly closes her eyes.
"Jesus is here with you, right now," the voice of the James jeans whispers, and a hand presses down on her head. "Can you see Him?"

She no longer dares to open her eyes, but something pearl gray and clear spills across the inside of her lids.

"I see a hem," she whispers.

"Christ has come and made you, Pirkko, his own," the James jeans say.
And when

I open my eyes, I'm surrounded by anoraks in a tight, smiling circle.

I've found God.

"How does it feel?" the James jeans ask hoarsely.

I don't know how to answer.
Somehow the last few feet to the summit have gone by in a flash, and I can't see anything at the top.
Even the life I've left behind in the valley is hidden beneath a merciful fog.

It's windy on Pitkäsilta Bridge, and the snow is mixed with stinging rain.
I try to hold on to Jesus Christ's hem since I've never been this close to God before.
And on the corner of Kirjatyöntekijänkatu and Pohjoisranta, I catch a glimpse of something pearl gray.
I give thanks and let joy flood my heart,

though a niggling doubt troubles me.

The James jeans gave me a rather long lecture about the primary responsibilities of someone who's been born again.

You must share your faith—not by preaching but by telling people about it when asked.
And there's no need to practice what to say beforehand, because He will provide you with the right words: when a person who believes in God speaks about their faith, it is really God, and not the individual person themselves, who speaks about Himself through that person.
You need to settle accounts with your old self and former life like Matthew did: he was a tax collector and later became an evangelist, and he returned all the tariffs he'd wrongly collected to their rightful owners.

Since it's a mere detail, I probably shouldn't ask how exactly he managed that.
A fleeting thought about the extra change I collected while the Moscow Circus was in town crosses my mind,

but I gather that the returning of money, in mine as in Matthew's case, is meant symbolically rather than literally.

Then the James jeans give me a direct order: I must ask for forgiveness from everyone I've ever sinned against right away.
This includes Father and Mother and Grandpa, as well as my friends and teachers, so in reality being born again doesn't feel nearly as simple and profound as I'd imagined it would as I stood among the rows of office binders.

But the final part of the speech is the hardest to accept:

"You increase in me, and I will decrease in you."

It means that I must make room for God's voice in me. The end result should be one where only God's voice issues forth when I open my mouth.

It's a requirement that feels entirely at odds with my desire to become a writer.
How can I enjoy the money and fame of being a writer if the books I write are solely the work of God?
Do I want someone to write my books on my behalf, even if that someone is God?

And the blood-curdling question:
Do I want to decrease?

Do I want to hand over the frail contours of my self to be trampled on by someone else?

I have the opportunity to try out my first requirement as soon as Airi and the kalakukko take the window seat on the 91 bus.

I tell Airi I've been born again.

Airi nods solemnly.
"Well, that can be a good thing. Or how do you see it? I can tell you that finding God has been the most wonderful and significant experience of my life," she says, warmly squeezing my hand in her own leather-gloved one.
"I'm so glad to hear you've found inner peace," she continues. "Don't we all just keep on spinning around and around in this hamster wheel called life, and it seems like you can't make any sense of it, no way and no how."

Airi and I marvel at my good luck all the way to the Herttoniemi police station until a doubt crosses Airi's mind.
"But now what's Reiska going to think about this? Do you think he'll be pleased? What do you think?"

Reiska has emptied the bottle of Leijona whiskey

hidden behind the Lenins and is busy opening a bottle of Johnnie Walker in honor of Airi and his title as director of finance.

"He's got a bit of a reason to celebrate," Mother says apologetically to Airi at the coffee table. "He's got himself a new title."
"I'm director of finance," Father says, pouring a whiskey for Airi, despite her protests, and spraying water from the siphon on top.
"So many economists are nothing more than gofers these days."
"Well then, congratulations to the new director," Airi says as Mother brings out the kalakukko that's been warming up in the oven.
"Now how are you supposed to cut this again?"
"I told Kekkonen, I told Matti, he's Urho Kekkonen's son and sits on our board… I told him he'd better get a move on with those subsidies," Father explains, and Mother's jaw clenches tighter than ever. "He's younger than myself… I asked him if he minded if I addressed him informally when we were in the sauna recently. He said he wouldn't…no, that he would…I mean he would like it if I addressed him informally. What's wrong with that? We're on the same page about things…if about nothing else then at least about the Soviet Union and Johnnie Walker in any case, so…"

Father talks the entire evening.

Love your fellow man! I command myself, and I decide to apologize to Father the next morning.

Airi yawns heartily on the couch.
The kalakukko yawns through its opened crust on the coffee table, and Mother fakes a yawn in Grandpa's armchair.
"Well, it's time for bed," Mother says briskly, gathering the coffee cups to take into the kitchen. "Then we'll have a nice day tomorrow."

I help Mother willingly and, between the sink and the refrigerator, blurt out my news:
"I've become a believer. I know it sounds strange, but…"
"Now help me get that drunk in bed," Mother whispers frantically. "We can talk about other things tomorrow."

The James jeans asked me if I pray.
I told him I actually pray all the time.
The James jeans thought that was a good thing and asked me what prayers I say.
I told him I don't say any particular prayers, that I usually come up with my own as I go.
The James jeans thought that was a bit questionable, and he suggested I say the Lord's Prayer, the one Jesus Christ taught his disciples himself, because it contains everything a person needs.
It may feel a little mechanical because it's so familiar, but if you take your time and stop to think carefully

BACKLIGHT

about the meaning behind each sentence, you won't need any other prayers.

I pray slowly, pausing often in the darkness. At least half an hour has passed since "hallowed be thy name," and I'm about to get to the obscure "lead us not into temptation" when I hear restless rustling sounds from Father's and Mother's side of the bedroom.
I stop praying.

"I wish you wouldn't, when Airi's here too," Mother whispers impatiently, and Father:
"It's money that makes the world go round. And let me tell you, it's the director of finance who makes the money go round."
Father's voice grows thicker and is drowned in vague panting.
I sit up. I can see Father's and Mother's blanket rising and falling rhythmically in the dim light.
And

she flushes red with rage.

Her parents are having sex right in the middle of her newly born prayer!

She never apologized to her parents for being the way she was.

And she never went back to the office on Hakaniemi Square where Jesus Christ appeared every Saturday evening to those who wanted to shed their previous self like an article of dirty clothing.
But

the power that unleashed obscenities and reeking images before God's eyes redeemed her, as did

God, whose quiet and incomprehensible laughter she could sometimes hear in the dark.

a room of my own

The smell is coming from under Grandpa's door.

It's a pungent, musty smell, and although I've never come across it before, I immediately sense danger.

The first time I notice it, we've just come out of the sauna, Mother and I, and our hair and minds are clean and pure.
"What is that?" I ask, but Mother hurries to open the balcony door and starts boiling water for coffee.
"We have to tell her at some point," Father says.
And

Mother tells me Grandpa has lung cancer.

The smell comes from garlic cloves Grandpa soaks in a lye made from birch ash.
Someone's got Grandpa believing that drinking the concoction can cure cancer.
I ask if Grandpa is dying, even though I know God is the only one who can answer a question like that—

and God isn't in the habit of answering.

Grandpa has to stop working at Solifer.
"For now." Grandpa says so himself, and we all eagerly repeat after him:
"For now."

Grandpa is there when I come home from school in the afternoons.
I make coffee and sandwiches with butter and bologna and then knock on Grandpa's door, the door that was supposed to seal me off from the rest of the family.

I don't want Grandpa's room anymore; I promise not to want it if Grandpa is allowed to live.
I don't want Grandpa's room if that means he has to die.
I don't want Grandpa's room at any price: not now, not ever.

We drink coffee and eat our sandwiches, Grandpa, me, and death, who's lurking in the corners.

We talk about the weather and Koski Hl., where Grandpa and Aunt Hilma and Aunt Helmi were born, and a little about hot water pipes, which Grandpa used to fix, and mopeds, which Grandpa fixed later on.

I'm afraid Grandpa will say something about death.

BACKLIGHT

I wish Grandpa would say something about death, because at the coffee table Grandpa's eyes wander and then stop suddenly.

"Look at that—a Eurasian blue tit."
I'm sure Grandpa is looking somewhere I can't, behind the thin curtain that separates me from death.
It's not until

six months after Grandpa's death that I find out Grandpa knew where he was headed as soon as he got the results from his first tests.
As Grandpa told his sisters, the ones who witnessed his birth in a cabin in the village of Kaunkorvi in Koski Hl., since the family didn't have a sauna; who saw him escape from their violent father by jumping over a non-existent gooseberry bush; who saw him sold as a farm-hand to the manor in the village of Hyvänneula, then escape to Helsinki to drive a horse-drawn cab and build his own house for his family in Mellunkylä, which was sold at auction when Grandma died and Tepsi had to be put down:
"I wouldn't have minded hanging on for a few more years."

Grandpa mourned Grandma's death by washing all the sheets with pine soap and cold water and hanging them on the wood pile to dry the night she died.
The next day Mother put the moldy sheets in the washer and threw in some Omo detergent, even though

Grandpa's message was as clear as V. A. Koskenniemi's elegy: "Alone you are, human being, alone you are in this world."

Grandpa ends up in Laakso Hospital in November and doesn't come home again until Christmas.

Grandpa wants to be the Finnish Communist Party's Santa Claus on Christmas Eve, just like he has every Christmas Eve since we moved to Puotila, and Father leads him from house to house so he can entertain everyone with his muddled rambling; on St. Stephen's Day, we put Grandpa in the Moskvitch and take him back to the hospital.

"Since he's just not up for it anymore," Father says.

I visit Grandpa regularly, every two or three days, despite Mother's protests:

"I don't think she should have to see everything just yet."

Grandpa lies in bed, just like I did twelve years ago when I had abdominal tuberculosis, and the rails make him think he's behind bars, just like I did:

"They put me in jail last night. They interrogated me all night, but I didn't confess to anything."

"He wants to get up so much," the nurse explains. "But he'll just end up unconscious on the floor if we lower the rails."

And we race to assure the nurse and the hospital that they're right to keep the rails up, Mother, Father, and I all do—we're not subject to coercive measures, at least not yet.

In February Mother suggests I move into Grandpa's room.

"He's not coming back, if we're being at all realistic," Mother says. "Not even to visit. I'm sorry to be so direct."

I refuse.

I join forces with Grandpa against death and the hospital, Father and Mother, and my own puberty.

And Grandpa responds to my call to arms with a brief flash of insight:
"You take care of yourself, you hear. You need to be healthy when you're young."
And

she takes these words, just as they are, and puts them in the mouth of an aunt on her deathbed in her debut novel, and later again in the TV movie version.
And she will forever be grateful to the director for not playing sentimental violin music in the background as this line is spoken.

In March, Grandpa sits on his bed with his hair sticking up and a baffling newly knitted cardigan at his feet, and he grabs empty air in his hand, offers it to Father:

"Here's this too, while I remember."
And

the next time I see Grandpa he's dead.

Grandpa is yellow and calm, and behind closed lids, his eyes see behind the curtain that separates me from death.

I press my lips to Grandpa's smooth, yellow forehead, and Mother and Father see the intentional ceremony in my action, they both do.
Father:
"Stop making such a fuss."
And Mother:
"I wish you wouldn't be so dramatic. This is serious."

We don't get an explanation for the newly knit cardigan at Grandpa's feet until we're back at the hospital entrance.

A well-dressed woman whose face powder is flaking comes up to shake our hands: first Father, then Mother, and finally me.
"Isn't it so terribly unfair that he had to leave us so soon?"

BACKLIGHT

I pray to God, whose existence I'm unsure of, that Father won't ask the woman to clarify her question.
But Father says:
"Well, soon and not. It's always too soon, but he did make it to a ripe old age, as we say."

The woman blinks rapidly; her powder flakes.

And now Mother prays with me, even though she doesn't believe in any gods at all as far as I know.
But Father goes on:
"He lived to see seventy-three, a decent age for a man these days."

And Father's the only one surprised to learn that Grandpa told his girlfriend he was getting ready for his sixtieth birthday celebration, for which his girlfriend knit the youthful cardigan she was hereby handing over to the deceased's family.

Now the room that was meant for me is mine.

I don't move in there until after Grandpa's funeral.

I sit in Grandpa's gray armchair, and I don't go into the living room to watch *The Untouchables* or *Ironside*.

I lie on Grandpa's bed with eyes closed and try to ward

off Grandpa's dreams, which don't belong to me.

I air out the room to get rid of the smell of birch ash lye and garlic, since the death of the person who died isn't mine.

And in late May, when the room has grown cold and damp as a monk's cell after being aired out for two whole months; when the blackbird has lamented the loss of its nesting tree on the odd-numbered side of Rantakartanontie; when the pale sickle moon has divided the sky into a right and left side, a right and wrong side—that's when Grandpa's dreams loosen their grip on me.

I have my own room for the first time in my life.

My thoughts collide with the walls and with other thoughts.
But the thoughts my thoughts collide with are my own, jumbled and capricious.
They're reflections of reflections.
And even though the walls can't stop my thoughts, dreams, and fears from escaping my reach, they leave traces, transparent signs in the air, which grows easier to breathe with each passing day.

I get out of bed, imprinted with the contours of my inaccessible self.
I'm ready to fight: to face Father and Mother and *Ironside* while holding on to my fragile, friable self.

BACKLIGHT

But the TV in the living room is silent.

The fountain murmurs, and Father and Mother are bent over the coffee table.
There's no coffee or coffee cups on the table, no sugar bowl or serving dish, no whiskey or soda siphon.
A large sheet of paper, stiff at the edges, is spread open across the table, and Father's finger glides solemnly along it.

And Father:
"I guess we ought to go ahead and tell her."

It's the floor plan of the apartment we're moving into: Father, Mother, and me.

"The countryside just doesn't suit a city guy like me after all," Father says.

The apartment doesn't exist, but the floor plan and the decision do.
The apartment is on Hämeentie; it will be.
"Not quite in Kallio but almost," Mother says, and Father:
"It's the Hermanni neighborhood, and it's got a very active branch of the Finnish Communist Pary. Right where Kallio and Sörnäinen meet."

She looks at the sheet of paper.

She is, and will continue to be, bad at looking at sheets of paper that show apartments devoid of all voices, smells, and colors.
But

she does see this: the apartment has only one bedroom. The apartment in Hermanni where Kallio and Sörnäinen meet is meant for two people.
"We can't count on you living with us that much longer," Mother says, and Father:
"I reckon you'll move into your own place at some point."
And

she looks at her parents in shock, because now she sees herself as her parents see her: a prickly burr stubbornly clinging to a hem eager to tear itself away.
And to her horror she suddenly sees her parents as they see themselves: a youthful couple living out the hottest heat of the day, freed of one dependent and already dreaming of the next one's departure.

I go stand in Grandpa's room.
It no longer belongs to Grandpa or me, doesn't even belong to Father or Mother.
It belongs to someone who's sitting at home bent over the floor plan of my home.

I no longer have a home.

BACKLIGHT

I stand in the room that has betrayed me, just like I do in the train station in the shadow of strangers, waiting for the train and fearing its arrival.

The Captainess passes the information along offhandedly as they're sitting by the edge of the pool, her own tanned legs splashing glistening drops of water in competition with the Captainess's blueish ones crisscrossed with varicose veins.

Tante Dolores is on the other side of the pool, and not even the wall of water formed by twenty splashing children can prevent her from seeing the look of malicious glee on Tante Dolores's face.

Tante Dolores hates her, and she understands Tante Dolores, and herself.

If she were Tante Dolores, she'd also hate the gap-toothed foreigner who separated her from her beloved and who now follows her around looking as if things could be put right.
I like Tante Dolores, even though she insists cold jars

of jam are hot, and even though she kicks the children with her soft slippers and steals their chocolate.
I like her because I can't *not* like her.
I can't avoid liking her because I don't know what Tante Dolores thinks of me.

She likes Tante Dolores because she's afraid of Tante Dolores's secret thoughts.
She's afraid Tante Dolores's thoughts will become flesh, just like the Captainess's thoughts have.

The Captainess tells me in German.
She says it with her neck, since her eyes are busy evaluating how likely it is the children will come down with a cold or an ear infection in the lengthening shadows of the cool August evening.
The Captainess doesn't want to see my expression when she tells me.

She says the car only has room for four people.

The car will be off to Lake Thun in a week, and the Captain and the Captainess, the tent and picnic baskets, and the rainwear and Kurt and Dorre will be in it.

The Captainess suggests that I take a day trip to Lake Thun on my own, by train and ferry, and eat the lunch the Captainess herself would prepare for me, which in addition to cold cuts would include lots of crusty bread and a jar of blackberry jam.

I nod, *sehr gern*, and for a moment my hands grope at nothing before they find the sturdy cotton hem of my Marimekko dress.
And

a hand appears from the right side of her peripheral vision, holding a damp sponge.
The sponge wipes the following images from her retinas:

The first image:

She and the Captainess sit on a rock by the shore as the sun sets over Lake Thun.
Dorre washes the camping dishes soiled by the delicious evening meal safely out of earshot.
Kurt does 600 push-ups and leaves them in peace, as does the Captain, who cheerfully patches the tire that was punctured on the mountain road.
And now that they finally have the opportunity for a leisurely chat, just the two of them, the Captainess would like to know what she thinks of Switzerland and the methods they employ at the orphanage, which, according to the Captainess herself, may be in need of reevaluation, and perhaps even a joint brainstorming session.

The second image:

The sun sets, Dorre washes the dishes, Kurt does his push-ups, and the Captain patches the tire.
The Captainess would like to go rowing on the lake, and as it so happens, they find a leaky rowboat between some rocks at the water's edge.
The Captainess is about to interrupt Kurt to ask him to take her out on the lake, since Kurt, as the Captainess proudly proclaims, has just returned from the army and knows how to row.
Barely concealing her modesty, she suggests that the Captainess not disturb Kurt and let her row instead.
The Captainess hesitantly agrees, and they row along the lake, which sparkles like a cold jewel amid the snow-capped Alps.
The Captainess is amazed and asks if all Finns can row. And in brilliant German, her voice thick with emotion, she paints a picture for the Captainess of a dark summer night where fog moves restlessly over the calm, black surface of a lake, a duck cries for its lost chick on a lonely lakeside rock, and far away, the smoke from a smoke sauna rises straight up into the sky—and even farther away there's the call of a cuckoo, a bird that doesn't even exist in Switzerland.

And the third image disintegrates in its own sentimentality:

The rowboat starts to leak, and the Captainess is

overwhelmed by the flood of water.

Panic-stricken, the Captainess screams for her son to save her, and he dutifully strips off his clothes and jumps in the water; but as he does so, he remembers that the mighty Swiss army doesn't teach its recruits how to swim.

She's the one who saves the Captainess, and that night, in the glow of the campfire, the Captainess thanks her for saving her life.

The Captainess gets up to wipe Adrian's runny nose with a tissue she finds in her sleeve, and she still doesn't look at me when:

"You could go tomorrow, early in the morning. Tante Dolores has promised to take care of house number three while you're gone. And afterward, too. Maybe you could spend the rest of your time here relaxing and just help out a little bit here and there."

And Tante Dolores, who couldn't possibly have heard the Captainess through the wall of water, smiles at me for the first time since Tante Irma's departure.

I've failed in my Pestalozzi/Julie Andrews/Summerhill approach to childrearing—I know that I have.

I've tried my best, and I know that, too.

In house number three I replaced the pictures depicting the torture of St. Sebastian and the one of St. Francis of Assisi babbling to the birds with the children's own drawings.

The Captainess thought it was a good idea, as she suspected Tante Sigfrid was secretly a Catholic.

I encouraged the children to draw their real thoughts on paper, and I only censored the slanders directed at the Captain's family, like the one where a giant penis pokes out from under Dorre's piano or the one where the Captainess stands atop a flattened Captain with a red crucifix in hand.

I met with the children to talk about the house rules, itself a concession, since the children at Summerhill School don't allow adults at their meetings.

I silenced my doubts about national differences playing a decisive role in the development of children's courage, initiative, and sense of responsibility, even though the children at Summerhill School have undeniably proven themselves to be more mature in making their own decisions than the Swiss children of Münsingen in house number three, who constantly push and shove each other, giggling with embarrassment.

BACKLIGHT

Nevertheless, under my leadership, the children unanimously decided that they would wake up on their own in the mornings, eat dinner only when they were hungry, do their homework only when they found it meaningful, and go to bed only when they were tired.

Blushing with embarrassment, I taught the children the song that's made such a deep impression on me: "Doe, a deer, a female deer; ray, a drop of golden sun; me, a name I call myself; far, a long, long way to run…"
I taught the children to sing it in a round,
but

as soon as I turned my back, the children made lewd gestures and came up with their own lyrics to the song in Swiss German, which I don't understand.
And the children were late for school; they suffered from headaches and nausea; they made messes in the kitchen with honey and instant coffee; they jumped on the sofa until the springs came out.
The children painted obscene pictures with my lipstick on the bathroom mirror; they tied French-speaking Brigitte to the coat rack for three hours; they tattled to the Captainess about their dirty clothes; they took turns climbing on Tante Dolores's lap to yawn and twirl her permed curls around their fingers.

The children said their prayers at morning tea, lunch, dinner, and bedtime without compulsion or religious conviction, and I've been forced to admit that caged animals don't want to be free.

She doesn't know if the lake she is crossing in a small ferry is Lake Thun—she doesn't have a map of Switzerland with her.

The morning is cold; it still is.
Frost advisory for low-lying areas, they'd say in the country she's from, a country she can never return to, not as she remembers it.
The lake is surrounded by hills, and their summits, to her disappointment, aren't covered in snow. Their steep sides are reflected in the oil-smooth water.
But

she doesn't see them.
She sees a mother and son,
because

her world, though she still hasn't realized it, is made up of people and the fragile connections between them: passing glances; faces ravaged or preserved in a state of waxlike immobility from lives lived in secret; words left unspoken; evasive and yielding gestures; endless guesses and fumbling interpretations.

The mother sitting across from her and deftly wielding her crochet hook is a warship in full sail, but her son

BACKLIGHT

has no rudder.

The woman is old for a mother, but she's clearly no grandmother because her eyes habitually follow the boy's movements, even though her ample rear end, covered in black polka dots, calmly weighs down the ferry's slatted bench, and her incredibly small and chubby hands produce a red and green scarf as ceaselessly as a sewing machine.
The boy, who looks to be about twelve and is as ready as Jesus Christ to answer the insolent questions put to him by wizened people, asks his mother with his eyes for permission to get up from the bench and carefully lean against the railing, letting the cool morning breeze blow out the back of his shirt as he looks out at the morning and the hills damp with dew.
And

she—the one who's been sent to Lake Thun to enjoy the majestic and unforgettable scenery—writes a story about the boy in her mind, a boy who is never disgraced by the tireless gaze of his overbearing mother and who finds salvation only when he falls in love with a woman who doesn't see with her eyes but with her soul.

She climbs up a mountain whose name she doesn't know.
But the mountain isn't in the Alps; she realizes as much

because the Alps are shimmering there in the morning sun, as unattainable as ever.

The terrain is brown and bumpy, and she tries not to notice she's out of breath.
She sees edelweiss and tries to be impressed.
But the edelweiss is small, hairy, and insignificant, and she doesn't dare pick it to remember it by, as it's blocked off by a green plastic cord tied to small stakes, and on the other side there's a cardboard sign attached to an iron wire that's been rinsed in the rain: *Verboten*.

She sits down on the mountaintop, dripping with sweat. Her skin, which no one has touched in months, hurts, as if it's been caressed too much.

She sits on the summit of her mountain, and as the fog moves restlessly over the summit opposite, she falls asleep without even eating the lunch the Captainess has packed for her; the sore skin on her back touches the wet, icy Swiss grass, and she has three dreams in a row.

I've bought a house.
The house is large, beautiful, and rundown, and it has no kitchen.
After searching for it for a long time, I find the kitchen downstairs.
The stove glows hot; I warm my hands in its warmth and fall asleep.

BACKLIGHT

I've bought a house and find a kitchen downstairs with a stove glowing red and hot.
I want to be alone, to warm my hands in the red glow of the stove, but I hear a commotion behind the kitchen doors.
The kitchen doors are old and fastened with old-fashioned hooks.
The noise intensifies, and the hooks begin to move on their own.
People who have no right to enter my kitchen are trying to get in.

I've bought a house, and I'd like to show it to Mother.
The house has three floors, and I'd like to show Mother the second and third floors.
The house has marble stairs, and it's located on Market Square because it's the Presidential Palace.
There's lots of gold, and palm trees bearing strawberries divide the hallways' marble walls.
On the second floor there's a café with golden walls and tomatoes growing from cracks in the floor; it's full of people I haven't invited.
Mother doesn't mind the people, but I do: I don't like that anyone at all can enter my house.
I want to go down to the basement, but Mother doesn't, and I don't want Mother in my basement either.
We stay at the café, and Mother eats a raspberry pastry as a choir begins to sing a song,
to which

she wakes up.

The fog has dissipated, and the mountain rising before her is stunning.
It's brown and steep, just like her own mountain, and it hides her view of the valley.
A choir dressed in Swiss national costumes is climbing her mountain, and they're singing a folk song in Swiss German that begins to make her dizzy.
Colorful skirts approach her; a sparrowhawk plunges from the cliff.

The mountain sways beneath her, and she's forced to cling to the fragile grass so she won't fall.
But the grass bends beneath her hands, tinkling like glass, and she falls and falls deep into a ravine.

The Swiss German song fades away.
She lies at the bottom of the ravine, and the brown mountains stoop down to stare at her as she sinks beneath the grass and the rocks and the gravel, beneath the earth's crust into the hot, heaving black magma within, and she finally gives up,
and

she can't understand how she's ended up in a white room with a view of thick green poplars and a pool shimmering in the sun.
She wakes to sharp knocks on the door, and before she can open her eyes, a tray with a bowl of soup, a glass of

juice, and a pile of worn letters is placed on the chair next to her bed.

Tante Dolores is already taking her leave when she opens her mouth to ask her to stay.

She has to find out how she ended up beneath the earth's crust and who Orpheus was, who was merciful and released her from the spinning, airtight realm of the dead.

But all that comes out of her mouth is a helpless whimper. Tante Dolores hesitates for a moment, but she turns her head after all:
"You're awake?"
"Thank you" slips out.
"Your fever seems to have gone down," Tante Dolores says and is about to leave again,
but

I have to make her stay.
I have to apologize to Tante Dolores, although I don't know what for.
"How is Tante Irma?" I ask randomly.
Tante Dolores doesn't smile.
"The Captainess asked me to give you these letters. She forgot to give them to you earlier."
"Where does Tante Irma live these days?" I ask,
and now

Tante Dolores smiles at her.
"And why does that interest you?"

There are nine letters, and three of them are from Mother.
I decide to open them last.
But I forget to open them,
because
the world is on fire.

Ketti's little sister has come back from America and reports that America is already burning.
It's only a matter of time before the Black Panthers take over, and then Black America will help Africa to rise up, with the help of Frelimo, of course.

Biafra is demanding independence, and my friends are demanding Biafra's independence on the streets of Helsinki in protests that have spread across the city, from Hakaniemi to Temppeliaukio Church, and here I am in a white room that has become my prison.
Jokke writes that people are standing up for democracy in Prague, in Munich, and in front of the Soviet embassy in Helsinki, just as they are in Paris, Rome, and everywhere progressive forces exist to support Dubček.
Vietnam and all of Latin America are protesting against U.S. imperialism, and students in Berlin, Paris, and Helsinki are demanding the "one man, one vote" principle at their universities. "We need everyone's support," writes Timppa, who's joined the Academic

BACKLIGHT

Social Democratic Society.

The streets are filled with protestors, red flags, slogans, and firebombs, and I'm sitting in this white room like a duck in a cardboard box.
The world is expanding like a helium balloon, and the songs of solidarity are wiping out the borders between countries because the era of nation states, religions, and racial differences is over.
And the world, whose very foundations are shaking in the newly risen storm, is somewhere else, beyond the window of this white room, but now, after having read these letters, I know it's waiting for me.

The world is a giant body with abscesses this already raging fire will burn away, just as my fever has burned away my doubts and God, who rotted my insides.

The poplars pant in the August heat.
The Captainess covers her head with a newspaper as the Captain teaches the newly arrived Dieter how to tie his shoelaces.
Tante Dolores brings the Captainess juice and lifts René onto her lap after he trips; she openly blows on his knee so the Captainess is sure to see it.

And suddenly I feel sorry for Tante Dolores, who never gets so much as a glance from the Captainess, not even when she brings her a glass of juice.

The Captainess is busy staring at her car, which Kurt is polishing, and now I feel sorry for her too, because Kurt never casts so much as a glance at her: he's focused on the calluses that have formed from his excessive strength training.

And I feel sorry for Dorre, who's playing Bach's preludes with spiritless precision behind the white curtains, and for the Captain, who will undoubtably be fiddling with shoelaces up until his retirement.

And I even feel sorry for the stagnant water in the swimming pool, which no one remembers to replace, and the houses that swallow children and were built to be modern but are already outdated.

House number three may be in the middle of Europe, but it's also in the middle of nowhere—and I'm the only one who can get out.

The children will grow up and leave in time, but the Captain and the Captainess and Tante Dolores, and probably Kurt too, will all stay behind, because they can't hear the silent, menacing tremors that are drawing near.

She stands by her window, but she's no longer here.
She probably never was, at least not during the past few months.

BACKLIGHT

She was sitting at her desk in winter, looking with unseeing eyes at the chalkboard where equations mysteriously assembled themselves.

No, her eyes weren't unseeing.
They saw the snow-covered Alps, stunning green valleys, and ponds in the woods aglow with ice crystals; they saw foggy Swiss mornings and clear Swiss evenings, just like

her eyes now see wild crowds, crumbling marble columns, and gold dust whirling in the air like dervishes; blood splattered and etched into walls; torches, processions, and smokestacks straight out of the movies; battleships, the Odessa Steps, and fields of wheat stretching as far as the eye can see, dotted with red flags just like the fields here are dotted with poppies.

It's 5 a.m. and the world is cast in gold.

Shimmering fog lies tangled in a stand of willows; the untroubled grass is beaded with dew.

She's backlit by the sun as I cross the meadow with burning feet.

She's standing on the far side of the meadow, waiting for me.
The sun has sprung up from the woods and is so dazzling I can't see her face.
But I recognize her by her demanding posture that's used to waiting.

Now she's waiting for me.

I'm not sure I want to see her.
So I stop to listen to the trill of an early yellowhammer.

She doesn't leave but shifts impatiently.

I pick a tall blade of melic grass and quickly turn it into a sentence: *The grass's dreams are short but deep.*

She stands before me, looking at me.
She wishes I would look at her—she thinks it's possible.

But this summer, which is only just beginning, and the thirty-two summers that separate me from her and her from me, belong to me alone.

My stillness conveys this to her, and before the sun slips into its mold, she lets me pass.
My hand brushes against hers, and I'm startled.
Her hand is dry, already wrinkled, like partially melted plastic.

I leave. And don't look back.

With a career spanning over 40 years, **Pirkko Saisio** is a celebrated author, actress, and director in her native Finland. She has been recognized with many awards, including the 2003 Finlandia Prize, Finland's most prestigious literary prize, for *The Red Book of Farewells*. Her broad literary output includes novels written under the pen names Jukka Larsson and Eva Wein as well as essays, plays, screenplays for TV and film, and even librettos for the ballet. She received her degree in acting from what is now called the Theater Academy in 1975, and she worked there as a professor of dramaturgy between 1997 and 2001. Most recently, she was nominated for the Finlandia Prize for her latest novel *Passio* (Passion, 2021); it is her seventh nomination, more than any other author.

Mia Spangenberg translates from Finnish, Swedish, and German into English. Her published translations include works by Finlandia-Prize-winning authors Mari Manninen and Pirkko Saisio and acclaimed children's book author and illustrator Marika Maijala. She was awarded the American–Scandinavian Foundation's 2023 Nadia Christensen Translation Prize for her translation of Pirkko Saisio's *Lowest Common Denominator* (Two Lines Press, 2024). She holds a Ph.D. in Scandinavian studies from the University of Washington, Seattle.

ALSO BY PIRKKO SAISIO

Lowest Common Denominator

The Red Book of Farewells